W9-BHZ-773

"You can let yourself out when you unclog the sink,"

David said. "Oh, and don't forget the pie."

"Never fear," Claire replied, seeing that her daughter, Katy, was already clutching the pie tin.

David's date rose gracefully from the table. "You certainly have a wonderful landlady," she said. "I hope you know how lucky you are. I have to make an appointment a month in advance just to get a light bulb changed."

"Yes, Claire's the best when it comes to fixing all the things I manage to break around here." David ruffled Katy's hair and bent down to give her a kiss on the forehead. "And she's got a great little helper, too. Good night, pumpkin."

Katy smiled up at him adoringly. " 'Night, Daddy."

"Daddy?" His date stared down at Katy with a kind of horror.

"Oh, yeah, I forgot to mention that," David said apologetically. "Claire's not only my landlady, she's my wife."

Dear Reader,

During this holiday season, as friends and loved ones gather for Thanksgiving, Silhouette Romance is celebrating all the joys of family and, of course, romance!

Each month in 1992, as part of our WRITTEN IN THE STARS series, we're proud to present a Silhouette Romance that focuses on the hero and his astrological sign. This month we're featuring sexy Scorpio Luke Manning. You may remember Luke as the jilted fiancé from Kasey Michaels's *Lion on the Prowl.* In *Prenuptial Agreement,* Luke finds true love . . . right in his own backyard.

We have an extra reason to celebrate this month—Stella Bagwell's HEARTLAND HOLIDAYS trilogy. In *Their First Thanksgiving,* Sam Gallagher meets his match when Olivia Westcott returns to the family's Arkansas farm. She'd turned down Sam's proposal once, but he wasn't about to let her go this time.

To round out the month we have warm, wonderful love stories from Anne Peters, Kate Bradley, Patti Standard— and another heart-stopping cowboy from Dorsey Kelley.

In the months to come, watch for Silhouette Romance novels by many more of your favorite authors, including Diana Palmer, Annette Broadrick, Elizabeth August and Marie Ferrarella.

The Silhouette authors and editors love to hear from readers, and we'd love to hear from *you.*

Happy reading from all of us at Silhouette!

Valerie Susan Hayward
Senior Editor

UNDER ONE ROOF
Patti Standard

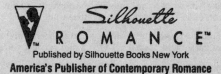

Silhouette
ROMANCE™
Published by Silhouette Books New York
America's Publisher of Contemporary Romance

If you purchased this book without a cover you should be aware that this book is stolen property. It was reported as "unsold and destroyed" to the publisher, and neither the author nor the publisher has received any payment for this "stripped book."

To my father,
who taught me, by example, to love books.

SILHOUETTE BOOKS
300 E. 42nd St., New York, N.Y. 10017

UNDER ONE ROOF

Copyright © 1992 by Patti Standard-Cronk

All rights reserved. Except for use in any review, the reproduction or utilization of this work in whole or in part in any form by any electronic, mechanical or other means, now known or hereafter invented, including xerography, photocopying and recording, or in any information storage or retrieval system, is forbidden without the permission of the publisher, Silhouette Books, 300 E. 42nd St., New York, N.Y. 10017

ISBN: 0-373-08902-3

First Silhouette Books printing November 1992

All the characters in this book have no existence outside the imagination of the author and have no relation whatsoever to anyone bearing the same name or names. They are not even distantly inspired by any individual known or unknown to the author, and all incidents are pure invention.

®: Trademark used under license and registered in the United States Patent and Trademark Office and in other countries.

Printed in the U.S.A.

Books by Patti Standard

Silhouette Romance

Pretty as a Picture #636
For Brian's Sake #829
Under One Roof #902

PATTI STANDARD

started her writing career after she stopped working full-time and began an at-home typing service. She says that the brand-new word processor and all those blank disks were too tempting to ignore. Having been a romance fan since her teens, she decided that the time would never be better to try to put on paper the stories she'd been writing in her mind for years.

Patti also loves to travel. She says that she started with Hawaii when she was sixteen and has been going ever since. Her family knows that trouble is brewing when she spreads out her map collection on the living room floor. She lives in a small town in western Colorado at the edge of the Rocky Mountains with her children and husband.

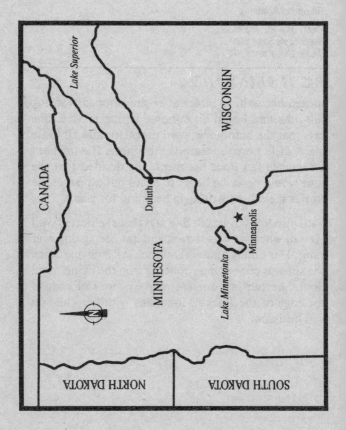

Chapter One

Claire didn't slam down the phone. She replaced the receiver slowly. Deliberately. With a click.

Her daughter looked up from the coloring book she had spread out on the kitchen table. "What'd he break this time?" she asked, laying down a red crayon and considering the color choices she had scattered before her.

"Not break—plugged," her mother answered briefly, already reaching for the coat hanging on a peg by the front door.

"The kitchen sink again?"

Claire Olson nodded, slipping her down-filled coat over her sweatshirt. April was still winter in Minneapolis and a bitter north wind had been making the old house creak all evening.

"I thought you told him to stop putting coffee grounds down the drain," the little girl said, finally deciding on a green crayon. Her thin legs began swinging rhythmically under her chair as she bent her head to her task once again, concentrating on staying in the lines.

"He swears he didn't." Claire struggled to start the zipper on her bulky coat. "Hey, Katy, run and get my toolbox, would you? I might have to take apart the P-trap again."

"Okay." The little girl dropped her crayon and obligingly slid off her chair. "You want the splunger, too?"

"Plunger," Claire corrected automatically. "Yeah, bring it, too." Silently she cursed the plumbing in the old house. This was the third time this month!

"Can I come up with you?" Katy asked hopefully. "Maybe he'll ask us to stay for supper."

"Now, don't you start that begging for food business!" Claire scolded. "I'll start supper as soon as we get back."

"What are we having?" Katy sounded suspicious.

"Your favorite. Fish sticks and—"

"Macaroni and cheese," the child finished with a groan. "Yuck."

"You love fish sticks!" Claire reminded her indignantly.

"Not every night!"

"Well, I guess we could have—"

"I know. I know. Scrambled eggs and toast." Katy sighed and went to fetch the toolbox from the hall closet.

She soon returned, trailing a plunger in one hand, and in the other carrying the battered red tackle box Claire had converted into a first-aid kit for a house with plumbing and wiring from before the Second World War. Her mother helped bundle her into her own small coat and tied the hood securely under her chin. Then they both took a deep breath of warm air, bracing themselves before opening the door, and stepped quickly into the freezing night.

Damn David, anyway! Claire grumbled as she left their ground-floor apartment and trudged up the set of stairs that ran along the outside of the old three-story house. Expecting her to come out on a night like this! Wishing she'd worn gloves, she shifted the tool-box into her other hand, the metal handle immediately beginning to freeze those fingers in turn.

All seemed quiet as they passed by the Captain's second-floor apartment. She hushed Katy, stopping her from bumping the plunger along each step as they climbed, in case her new, early-rising tenants had already gone to bed. It looked as though the Captain and his wife were going to be good tenants, she thought as they tiptoed past the door. A little eccentric, but they paid their rent right on time.

She found her teeth clenching as she reached the converted apartment on the third floor. The smell of charcoaled steak was seeping around the edges of the closed door in front of her, making her empty stomach growl, and the dim, flickering light casting shadows against the curtains could only be coming from those tapered, scented candles he always liked to use when he was wining and dining a woman.

Oh, great! Claire thought to herself as she rapped sharply on his door. Calling her up to fix his sink when he had a woman with him! Which was most of the time!

It was a blonde tonight, Claire noted as the door was opened and she could see into the room. Pretty hot stuff, too, she thought, shooing a pink-cheeked and windblown Katy ahead of her into the warmth of the darkened apartment. The woman was seated at the table, wineglass in hand, and the siren-red nails wrapped around its stem were visible even from a distance, matching the color of a slinky dress with a neckline that gave new meaning to the word cleavage.

Claire's hand automatically went to the light switch next to the door. She felt a brief moment of satisfaction when she saw that the blonde didn't look quite as glamorous squinting under the sudden glare of a one hundred-watt bulb as she had bathed in scented candlelight.

"Boy, Claire, you sure know how to ruin a mood!" David said from behind her, squinting as his eyes tried to adjust to the bright light.

"I've always had trouble unclogging sinks by candlelight," she replied, her tone withering. "Silly me."

But her tenant just grinned at her as he pushed the door shut against the wind. Turning to Katy, he reached down and picked the child up, twirling her high in the air. "Hey there, princess!" he said. "Your mom has a wicked tongue on her, you know that?"

"Momma said we have to be firm with you," Katy responded seriously, settling herself comfortably on his hip.

"Is that so?" David's grin became even more wicked. "Well, she's probably right."

Claire shot him a look while she shrugged out of her coat, dropping it on the sofa as she made her way through the living room and over to the sink in the kitchen, giving the blonde no more than a polite nod as she passed the table.

It was harder to ignore the remains of what had obviously been an excellent dinner spread out on the oak tabletop. The two plates were swimming in au jus, reddened from what she was sure had been perfectly grilled medium-rare steaks. The blonde had left the skin from her baked potato uneaten, and it laid there on the edge of her plate, still decorated with golden butter and snowy-white sour cream. And almonds! He'd sprinkled the julienne-cut green beans with little slivers of almonds!

Lordy, but the man could cook! Claire had to admit as she dropped the toolbox onto the counter and pried open the lid.

"So what'd you put down it?" she asked, grabbing a long-handled screwdriver and trying to peer through several inches of standing water to see into the dark hole at the bottom of the sink.

"Lettuce leaves, I swear! Just lettuce leaves from the salad." David stood close behind her, peering over her shoulder. "The disposal ate them right up, I thought, but the next time I turned on the faucet—there you have it." He watched with interest as she began poking the blade of the screwdriver down the garbage disposal, feeling for a stray piece of silverware or some other object that might be jamming the blades. With David, you never knew what you might find.

"Davey, aren't you going to introduce us?" A low, throaty voice sounded behind them.

Uh-oh, Miss Cleavage needs some attention, *Davey*, Claire thought to herself, hiding a smile.

"Melinda, darling, I'm sorry!" David sounded genuinely contrite and moved instantly to her side. "This is Claire, my landlady," he said, gesturing to where Claire stood leaning over the sink. "And this is my little princess, Princess Katy. And this, this must be her scepter," he teased, indicating the plunger she still held in her small hand. He gave the giggling little girl on his hip a kiss on the nose and let her slide down to the floor so he could begin helping her out of her coat.

"Ladies, this is Melinda," David introduced. "She's an aerobics instructor at my health club."

Claire smiled at the woman thinly, determined not to feel frumpy even if she was about six inches shorter and was dressed in faded blue jeans and a sweatshirt that had seen better days.

"Hi," she said.

"Hi," Katy echoed.

"Hi." Melinda's greeting was no more original.

Well, that took care of the pleasantries, Claire thought, turning her attention back to the sink. Let *Davey* keep the conversational ball rolling.

But conversation had always been David's specialty. The man could charm a snake, Claire thought, flipping on the disposal switch, listening to the blades hum happily, although they didn't lower the level of the standing water by so much as an inch. Sighing, she took the plunger from Katy and made a few tentative swooshing jabs while she listened to David alternately flatter Melinda and tease Katy.

He did have a way with women, she had to admit that. Grocery clerks, meter maids, bank tellers, even the little old ladies who rang the bells over the Christmas charity pots—one and all, within minutes David would have them smiling, feeling ten years younger and twenty pounds lighter.

"Here, princess, have a piece," she heard him saying now to Katy. She looked over to see Katy standing by the table, her chin almost resting on its top, looking longingly at a half-eaten apple pie just inches from her nose. David was reaching for a knife to cut the child a wedge.

"She hasn't had supper yet," Claire interrupted, her tone sharper than she intended. She knew the pie would have a crust that would almost melt in your mouth—she could feel the saliva forming at the mere thought of it. She also knew that compared to the aerobics instructor, lithe and taut and disgustingly fit, she probably looked like a stuffed sausage. One slice of that pie had at least seven hundred calories. David always used real butter, she thought with a pang.

"Well, take it home and save it for after supper then," David suggested amicably. "What are you having? Fish sticks or scrambled eggs?"

"Fish sticks," Katy responded morosely.

"Ahh." David's tone was knowing.

Tight-lipped, Claire worked the plunger furiously up and down in the sink, causing water to slosh dangerously. So what was the matter with fish sticks? They were quick, nutritious and didn't have that annoying habit of burning on the outside while the inside stayed determinedly raw, as did so many things she tried to cook. The same went for scrambled eggs.

"If you'd preheat the oven, Claire, your fish sticks wouldn't get quite so rubbery, you know," David commented helpfully.

"Thanks for the tip." Claire didn't sound at all grateful.

"Well, we'd better get going if we want to make that movie in time," David said heartily, moving behind Melinda to help pull back her chair.

"Movie?" Melinda echoed. "But I thought we were going dancing. I'm a little over-dressed for a movie, don't you think?"

David eyed the clingy red dress, the low neckline and vampy material clearly registering on him for the first time. Realizing his unflattering mistake, he said smoothly, "I think you look luscious, and I can't wait to show you off on the dance floor."

Melinda positively purred up at him, all forgiven, and once again Claire was left shaking her head in amazement at the way women fell for his line.

"Claire, you can let yourself out when you get that thing clear, can't you?" David asked. "Oh, and don't forget the pie."

"Never fear," Claire replied, seeing that Katy was already clutching the pie tin carefully in front of her.

Melinda rose gracefully from the table, standing beside David with one hand resting lightly on his arm. "You certainly have a wonderful landlady," she said.

"I hope you know how lucky you are. I have to make an appointment with my building's manager a month in advance just to get a light bulb changed."

The compliment sounded sincere, causing Claire to turn her head to give Melinda a closer look. She looked fairly intelligent, after all, Claire had to admit. She knew David didn't usually date vapid women, no matter how great a shape they were in.

"Yup, Claire's the best when it comes to fixing all the things I manage to break around here." He ruffled Katy's hair and bent down to give her a kiss on the forehead. "And she's got a great little helper, too. Good night, pumpkin. I love you."

Katy smiled up at him adoringly. "'Night, Daddy. I love you, too."

"Daddy?" Melinda's eyes widened and she stared down at Katy with a kind of horror.

"Oh, yeah, I guess I forgot to mention that," David said apologetically. "Claire's not only my landlady, she's my wife."

"Your wife?" The poor woman had paled noticeably at that and was looking rather wildly at Claire now.

"Ex-wife!" Claire corrected firmly, taking pity on her. "*Ex*-wife. David has a rather weird sense of humor sometimes."

"Hey, you divorced me, I didn't divorce you."

"Now cut that out, David!" Claire ordered. "Don't worry, Melinda, we've been divorced for almost two years now. He's a free man. Warped, but free."

"You live in the same building as your ex-wife?" Melinda asked weakly.

"Got to stay close to my little princess, don't I?" David demanded reasonably. "Can't have her growing up behind my back and running off with some frog, now, can I?"

Katy giggled at that while David managed to get a still worried looking Melinda into her coat and out the door, waving goodbye unconcernedly.

I bet he has some fun evening now, Claire thought to herself, giving the plunger one more determined push. Just as the door clicked shut behind the departing couple, the drain made a gurgling burp and the water began to whirl down it with a loud, sucking sound.

"Hey, you did it!" Katy congratulated her, putting down her precious pie and dragging a chair over to the counter next to her mother so she could watch the water run freely down the drain.

Satisfied that the sink was unclogged—for now anyway—Claire closed the toolbox and helped Katy hop down from her chair. Turning from the sink, she was face-to-face with the table, still laden with dishes, the congealing food not appearing nearly so appetizing now. Typical David, she thought. Just walk off and leave the mess. "I'll worry about it later," could have been his motto during the five years of their marriage. And he hadn't changed one bit during the two years since their divorce!

"Don't worry," he'd say when she'd show him a stack of unpaid bills. "Don't worry," he'd say when she'd ask him if he'd had a reply from some magazine that he'd submitted a story to. "Don't worry" had the immediate effect of making her very worried indeed, a Pavlovian response that would cause an instant throbbing in her temples.

Claire crossed over to the table and blew out the sputtering candles. Absently she began stacking the dishes, automatically doing as she'd done so many times during her marriage, after so many meals, clearing the dishes away as her fair share of the housework—she did the dishes since David had cooked the meal.

With Katy's help, they had the kitchen cleaned and dishwasher loaded in short order. After punching the button to start the machine, Claire reached for a dish towel to dry her hands and stood surveying the room, her gaze moving from one piece of furniture to another, from the still life over the sofa to the hook rug under the coffee table. They were all familiar things, things that had once decorated the home she had shared with David—the home just two floors below.

She looped the dish towel through the handle of the refrigerator, and her eyes were caught by the little magnet on its door holding what appeared to be David's shopping list. She remembered that magnet: it was shaped like a heart with the name Claire printed on it. What in heaven's name was he doing with that old thing? she wondered in exasperation. They'd bought it on their honeymoon from a little gift shop on the beach. She hadn't given it a thought in years.

It was strange how things split up in a divorce. David got the still life and the heart magnet, Claire ended up with all the ashtrays—although she didn't smoke—and his grandmother's wedding picture. Strange.

Claire sighed, taking her eyes from the magnet and looking around for Katy. The soft sound of humming reached her ears, coming from the bedroom David kept for his daughter, filled with her own toys and clothes, since she often spent the night with him.

The childish lullaby drifted down the hallway toward the kitchen, and Claire felt her lips curve into a small smile as she listened to the tune. The gentle sound of Katy humming to herself relaxed Claire, allowing her to release muscles that she hadn't realized were tense. Any dealings with David seemed to leave her tense these days. Ever since he'd gotten that stupid idea of his! That ridiculous notion he'd cooked up that they should try to get back together again. Subtly, but determinedly, he'd been increasing the pressure lately, and she felt constantly on guard, trying to steel herself against his little hints and innuendos, his constant references to the ''good old days'' of their marriage. Good old days! Hah!

She straightened her shoulders and picked up the toolbox, crossing the living room to place it on the floor next to the door. Then she turned down the hall to fetch Katy. It was time they got going.

But as she passed the open doorway to David's bedroom, Claire automatically glanced in—and was stopped dead in her tracks. When had he put that back? She thought he'd taken it away ages ago and stored it in some bottom drawer where it belonged! She took a few steps into the room, staring at the photograph on David's nightstand. Her own face smiled back at her from the frame, a face young and happy, and oh, so confident. She was cradling a baby

Katy in her arms, standing beneath the old flowering crab-apple tree that still shaded the backyard of the house.

That tree had been the main reason they had bought the huge, three-story house. It had been in full bloom the first time they'd seen the house, its bright pink blossoms an explosion of color, and they'd talked about how their children would love to play among its gnarled branches. Of course, the house had been too big and too old, a white elephant the real estate agent was only too eager to let them have at a bargain-basement price. But they'd been attracted to the quiet little neighborhood with its slightly seedy homes carefully tended by elderly owners, the narrow street lined with shade trees so tall their branches met overhead to form a green tunnel in the summer.

They'd had so many plans for the house then. It had already been divided into apartments, but they'd been going to restore it to its original floor design—turning the upstairs back into bedrooms for all the children they were going to have.

Of course, they'd never gotten around to the remodeling, growing dependent on the rental income the two apartments provided. They'd never gotten around to all the children, either. And one by one the elderly owners next to them had died or moved in with relatives, putting their huge old houses on the market to be snapped up by yuppie couples eager to move to the suburbs to raise their children, spending their weekends in a frenzy of painting and insulating, turning the old neighborhood into one of the trendiest addresses in Minneapolis.

Claire's brow drew into a frown as she stared at the photograph. Why couldn't David face reality? That picture was of a time that was no more—of a Claire and a Katy that were no more. There had been years of growing disillusionment, of passionate arguing, of lengthening silences between the time that picture had been taken and now. There had been two years of *divorce!* Claire wanted to shout at him in sudden frustration.

But David simply refused to come to terms with their divorce. He insisted on living in a world as fiction-filled as the stories he wrote. Introducing her to his date as his wife, for God's sake! Why was it so hard for him to accept the fact that their marriage couldn't work? Ever!

"Mom! Mom, I'm starving to death!" Katy's impatient voice coming down the hallway jarred Claire back to reality. She was still standing frozen in David's bedroom, her eyes locked on the woman staring out of the frame at her.

"Okay." Her voice was small and tight. She tried again, louder this time. "Right, let's get going," she called, managing to sound her normal, brisk self. She turned sharply and walked out of the room, shutting the door behind her, vowing to get David a new picture of just Katy to put by his bedside.

Back in their own ground-floor apartment, unburdened of their coats and plumbing paraphernalia, Claire and Katy stood together in front of the refrigerator, looking glumly at the package of fish sticks Claire had just removed from the freezer.

Unenthusiastically, Claire tore open the box and dumped the frozen shapes onto a tray. Turning over the box, she searched the instructions to find the oven temperature. There it was. "Preheat oven to four hundred and fifty degrees." Preheat. Damn, David was right.

She tapped the box on the counter distractedly while she calculated. At least fifteen minutes to get the oven up to four hundred fifty degrees, another twenty minutes to bake the fish sticks, thirty-five minutes altogether... her stomach rumbled hungrily.

That settled it! Dumping the hard lumps unceremoniously back into their box, Claire returned them to the freezer. "Katy," she ordered, "get out a couple of plates." Rummaging through the refrigerator, Claire pulled out a carton of milk. "Glasses, too," she called, grabbing the package of cheddar cheese.

Moments later, she stood with Katy next to the table surveying the plates in front of her with satisfaction. "There! What do you think?"

"For supper?"

"Sure! Apples are nutritious, right? A glass of milk, a chunk of cheese, a big piece of your dad's scrumptious apple pie—I'd say we covered most of the basic food groups, wouldn't you?"

"All right, Mom!" Katy exclaimed, scrambling onto a chair and pulling one of the plates to her.

"And don't you *ever* tell your father about this!"

"Never," Katy agreed, her mouth already full of pie.

Later, stomachs satisfactorily filled, Claire helped Katy with her bath then tucked her into bed. Several stories later, Claire was finally able to say good-night and head for her own room and the long, hot shower she'd been looking forward to ever since she'd been forced to go out into the freezing night air.

Not that *he* ever gave a thought to things like catching pneumonia, Claire thought as she dried herself off and stepped into a pair of lace-edged panties. David's mind never considered the practicalities of runny noses or sore throats. Those were the kinds of things he always left for dependable, responsible Claire to deal with. He never considered the consequences of his actions, he—

Claire abruptly reined in her accusing thoughts. What had gotten into her tonight? she asked her reflection in the dresser mirror as she opened a drawer to get a clean nightshirt. She sounded as if she were a bitter, vengeful divorcée—something she'd sworn she'd never become.

Claire pulled an extra large T-shirt over her head and reached for a comb to run through her wet hair. Of course David had his faults, but she certainly had her share, too. If it took two to make a marriage, it sure as hell took two to make a divorce! Standing there cursing the man only reopened old wounds—just made everything worse.

It was probably seeing that picture by his bed, Claire acknowledged to herself, that had started her remembering this way. She'd been so young then, and so much in love. She dropped the comb onto the dresser top and leaned forward to peer at her face closely in the mirror. Did she look as old as she felt? Did her face show its twenty-eight physical years—or did it reflect the extra decades she felt mentally?

Actually, Claire had to admit, she didn't look too bad for a woman pushing thirty. She still turned a few male heads now and then. Of course, with her coloring she tended to stand out in this Minnesota city peopled by tall blondes of Scandinavian ancestry.

Claire's great-grandmother had been Hawaiian and her great-grandfather was a Scot, bequeathing to Claire a dramatic combination of thick black hair, emerald-green eyes with a slight tilt to the edges and the creamy white skin of an English maiden. She stepped back from the mirror and turned sideways, taking a deep breath and holding in her stomach muscles. Not bad. She was definitely short by Minneapolis standards, and she couldn't indulge in pie for supper too often, but she'd take her feminine curves over Melinda's anorexic aerobicized frame any day, she decided.

A smile softened her mouth. David always teased that she had the body of a hula dancer—hiding the soul of a librarian. Actually Claire had always considered her rather exotic looks to be a curse. Looking like a hula dancer tended to attract men who liked exotic women. Men looking for excitement and adventure. The very type of man Claire didn't want. Maybe if she'd been a little plainer, a little mousier, then she would attract the solid, dependable men she was looking for—instead of bums!

A knock on the door interrupted her self-examination. Claire glanced at the clock on her nightstand. Ten-thirty. She padded barefoot through the living room, flipping on a table lamp as she went. She didn't bother putting her eye to the peephole. She knew who it was.

"Go home!" she commanded as she pulled open the door.

"Ah, Claire, I don't want to go home. How about we make love instead?"

Chapter Two

"**No.**"

David stood on her doorstep, hands stuffed into the pockets of his coat. His blond hair was being riffled by the chill wind and he shifted from foot to foot in an effort to keep warm.

"Come on, darling! It's freezing out here! Let's go to bed." It was David at his most outrageous, but Claire wasn't swayed in the least.

"You can't come to my door reeking of another woman's perfume and expect to just fall into my bed. Go home!" She started to shut the door, but his hand shot out, holding it open.

"Now, how can you tell if I'm reeking from way in there?"

Claire sighed in exasperation. She hated it when he got in this mood. She also hated standing next to an open door in nothing but a T-shirt and panties, while the cold air washing over her made it abundantly clear she wasn't wearing a bra. And naturally David was noticing, his eyes watching with unconcealed interest while her nipples hardened and thrust against the thin cotton cloth.

Taking advantage of her moment's hesitation, David quickly pushed the door open farther and stepped inside, crowding up close to an unyielding Claire who was still trying to hold her ground. "There. Am I reeking?" he asked, pulling her against him.

Claire wrinkled her nose. "Yes. And you're cold! Get off me!" She placed her hands on his chest and pushed ineffectively.

His response was to move back just enough to smoothly unzip his coat and then, replacing his hands around her waist, he snuggled her into the warmth of his thick, cable-knit sweater.

"That better?" he asked, totally ignoring her still-pushing hands. He sniffed the air delicately. "Say, I have a great idea! How about I dab on some of that orange blossom stuff you're wearing? That should cover up my reeking. Then can I just fall into your bed?"

Claire managed to wriggle away from him slightly, throwing back her head to look up at him, green eyes sparkling with equal amounts of amusement and irritation. "For your information, I'm not wearing any perfume—that's my shampoo."

"Now that's an idea!" One of David's hands moved up to twirl a long dark strand of her still-wet hair. "Why don't we take a shower together? We haven't done that in years! You can shampoo orange blossoms into my hair and I'll do yours—I'll wash your back and you can wash mine—I'll wash your—"

"David!" Claire slapped his hand away from where it had slid down to rest on her bottom, lifting the edge of her nightshirt to caress the wisp of nylon underneath. She managed to twist from his grasp and headed toward the living room, but she was half smiling now.

David followed her as she went, watching closely the way her T-shirt slid up ever so slightly as her hips moved, revealing the barest hint of lace. "Don't be such a prude, Claire," he chastised, letting his eyes follow the length of her smooth legs down to her bare feet. "No matter what our differences, you have to admit, sex was not one of them."

"True," Claire agreed, lowering herself onto the sofa and tucking one foot underneath her. "But you should have thought of satisfying all these carnal desires while you were out with Goldilocks."

David shrugged out of his coat and tossed it along the back of the sofa. Pushing aside a decorative pillow, he sat down next to her, stretching out his long legs on the coffee table in front of them. "Oh, I thought about it, all right," he told her. "But I'm afraid Melinda and I just weren't meant to be." He tried to look sorrowful.

"What did you expect!" Claire snorted. "After announcing you were practically married! It's hard enough finding a man who doesn't go on and on about his ex-wife, let alone one who pretends he's still married!"

"You divorced me. I didn't—"

"I know! I know!" Claire interrupted the familiar refrain with exasperation.

"And besides—" He reached out and pulled her to him, liking the way it felt as she settled comfortably in the crook of his shoulder. "And besides," he repeated, "Melinda doesn't smell like you." He brushed his cheek against her glossy hair, filling his lungs with her scent. "She doesn't feel like you. And, I suppose if I'd bothered to kiss her, I'd have found out she doesn't taste like you, either." His tone had completely lost its banter. "And I want you."

"Damn it, David! Stop that!" Claire jerked upright, shifting away from him until she was wedged against the cushions in the corner of the sofa. She was dead serious now. He knew how much she hated him talking that way. Teasing was okay—but not this!

"Sorry," David apologized, immediately backing off, cursing himself. He knew he'd crossed Claire's invisible line, that he'd pushed too hard against the door she kept firmly shut against his repeated attempts at getting close to her again.

He forced a note of lightness back into his voice. "It wasn't what you'd call an entertaining evening. She spent the whole night talking about her work."

"Really?" Claire asked with a show of interest, trying to relax again, allowing David a graceful retreat. "I guess a whole night of aerobics could get sort of boring—after you've figured your resting heart rate, and all that."

"Not aerobics," he corrected. "That's just on weekends. Melinda's a professor at the college—American Lit."

"Uh-oh!"

"Yeah. She spent the entire evening critiquing my book."

"Ahh." Claire nodded sympathetically. She could imagine how that had gone over! David did *not* take criticism well.

"Regardless of the fact that it's number one on the *New York Times* bestseller list this month, our Melinda seemed to rate it quite a bit lower." He reached over and picked up her hand where it had been resting on one leg, and began to play idly with her fingers while he regarded her silently for a moment. "I wondered what had happened to my favorite T-shirt," he said absently, eyeing the cartoon drawing on her nightshirt, thinking to himself that the fat orange cat curving over her breasts and stomach was one lucky animal. "So he gets to sleep with you, but I don't?"

This time David made sure his voice struck just the right note. After two years, he was normally pretty good at this flirting-right-on-the-border-of-serious attitude that Claire forced him to take. Sometimes he slipped when, like tonight, she looked so sexy and desirable, the lamp making a soft halo of light around her hair, casting her face in mysterious shadows. But he knew from past experience that those kind of mistakes only pushed her farther away from him.

"We're old friends," Claire was saying, unaware of the self-control David was exercising. "I'm very selective about who gets in my bed."

"So I've heard," he responded dryly.

"David!"

"We both know very well that I was the first man to ever make love to you—and the last."

"How do you know so much about my love life?" Claire demanded indignantly. "You haven't been in my bedroom in two years. And not for lack of trying, I might add!" She pulled her hand out of his and crossed her arms stubbornly over her chest.

"It so happens I have my own little spy," he told her smugly.

"That's pretty low—pumping a *child* for information!" Claire ignored the twinge of guilt that assailed her, knowing she'd used Katy for the same purpose many a time. "Besides, you shouldn't believe everything a five-year-old tells you," she added, trying to look secretive.

But she knew David saw right through her. He was right, of course. David was her first, last and only lover. And, unbelievable as it seemed, Claire suspected that, like herself, David had had no other lovers since their divorce.

She stared at him now, thinking how handsome he was in profile, so Nordic looking with his high cheekbones, straight nose and square chin. His blond hair needed a trim, as always; curling slightly where it met the ribbed collar of his sweater. And his eyes, his ice-blue eyes, were even bluer tonight, enhanced by the blue tones of the sweater he wore.

Claire knew those were the eyes of a charming, sensitive, terribly romantic, ridiculously idealistic man. A man who wouldn't sleep with a woman unless he was deeply involved with her. And from watching the parade of women going up and down the stairs to the third floor—and from information cheerfully supplied by Katy—Claire knew he had never dated one woman long enough in the last two years to form the kind of attachment that would lead to physical intimacy.

Claire found her gaze traveling downward, fastening on to his mouth with its sensually full lips. Unwittingly she was reminded of the many times those lips had covered hers, coaxing responses from her that no other man had even approached—before or since. She hated thinking of those lips meeting another woman's. She was fiercely glad he hadn't kissed the provocative Melinda tonight. She found her free hand clenching and forced herself to take a deep breath, letting the air out slowly as she consciously uncurled her fingers.

David heard the long sigh and wondered at its cause—and worried about its cause. His little spy had been reporting some unsettling information lately. Not that he believed for a moment Claire's hint that she might be sleeping with someone, but still...

"Katy tells me you've been seeing a lot of Lawrence, lately," he mentioned casually.

Too casually. Claire was instantly alert.

"I'm doing the books for all three of his stores now," Claire answered carefully. "So I see quite a bit of him."

"I meant socially."

"Well, I suppose so, yes."

"Claire, we have to talk," David said suddenly, urgently. He half turned to face her, his blue eyes glittering intently.

"Oh, no, David! Not that again!" Claire jumped to her feet, shaking off his attempt to grab her arm. "Do you want something to drink?" she asked brightly. "Tea? Coffee?" She almost ran toward the kitchen.

"Claire—"

"Hot chocolate? That ought to take the chill off."

"Claire—"

She had picked up the kettle and was filling it with water, standing at the sink with her back to him, the faucet on full force.

Following her into the kitchen with impatient strides, David reached out to turn off the noisy faucet. He pried the kettle from her fingers and set it on the counter. Then, placing a hand on each shoulder, he forced her around.

But Claire wouldn't lift her eyes to his. Her shoulders drooped and the stiffness went out of her spine. What was the point of all this? she thought tiredly. They'd been over it so often before. She could almost guess his next words.

"Claire, I *need* you!" He was right on cue.

"You *say* you do," she countered woodenly.

"And you need me!"

"*Needed* you. Past tense!"

"Claire, it's been two years and we're both still right here—together! Can't you admit by now that we were meant to be?" he insisted, totally ignoring her qualifications.

Claire was silent, still staring at the floor.

"Well?" David demanded after a moment, seeing she wouldn't speak.

"Well, what?"

"Well, what's the problem, Claire?" His despair was obvious.

"What's the problem?" Claire repeated in amazement. "What's the *problem?*" Her eyes did meet his now, a tiny spark of anger she couldn't prevent making her voice rise ever so slightly.

"In the storybooks, two people meet, they fall in love, they live happily ever after!" David told her, the hands on her shoulders shaking her gently in his frustration.

Storybooks! Claire found her anger going up another notch. "You're the one who writes the storybooks, remember, David! Not me!" she snapped.

"And just what's that supposed to mean?" he demanded, rising to the bait, responding to her anger in spite of himself.

"What that means is that it takes more than falling in love to live happily ever after!" She twisted away from him, suddenly hating the possessive feel of his hands on her.

"More? For God's sake, Claire, what more is there?"

"You don't know, do you! You never understood what else a marriage needed! You never figured out the difference between *falling* in love and *being* in love!" Claire's anger had gone from a spark to a blaze. "The trouble with you is you end all your stories with 'and they lived happily ever after.'" Her voice mimicked his. "You never move past that! You need to write a sequel, David! You need to try to imagine all the other things that can happen to your characters after you write The End.''

She was breathing quickly now, old angers building, welling up, long suppressed feelings rising of their own volition as she tried to find words to express what had been missing from her marriage—all the other things she had needed.

''What about companionship?'' she demanded, unable to stop the angry torrent of words. ''What about sharing? What about having the same hobbies? The same friends? How about good, old-fashioned friendship, David?'' Claire slammed an open palm down on the counter for emphasis, confronting him, challenging him.

''Friendship?'' David repeated incredulously as she paused in her tirade, glaring up at him. ''You want us to be...friends?''

''For starters!'' she shot back.

But he was shaking his head at her, the shadow of a smile lifting the corner of his mouth. ''Claire, you know very well we can never be friends.''

David moved to close the space she'd tried to put between them, pushing her back until she was pinned between the counter and his body. ''Never friends,'' he repeated softly, raising a hand to her cheek, his thumb beginning to trace the outline of her bottom lip.

And Claire knew he was right. And she knew why. And she *hated* it! She tried to suppress the tremble that passed through her body at David's touch, not wanting him to see that he still had that power over her. But the slight narrowing of his eyes betrayed his triumph.

He knew! And he gloried in what happened when he touched her, increasing the pressure of his thumb as it left her lips and traveled along her jaw, brushing the length of his fingers along her cheek as he went.

Absolutely unable to stop herself, Claire turned her head to bury a kiss on his palm. She heard his sharp intake of breath as her lips moved across the sensitive flesh, but she felt no triumph of her own. This—this *passion* that flared between them, this uncontrollable passion was what made it impossible for them to ever be friends. How could something as gentle as friendship grow in this blast furnace of emotions that erupted at their slightest touch?

Although her hands had somehow managed to clasp themselves around his neck, although her lips had raised to meet his, although her heart beat in a matching staccato rhythm, still a part of her mind was chanting, over and over again, no, no, NO!

This was how every argument they had ever had had ended. This blissful coupling had solved their every problem. Yet the problems had never really been solved. They had only been temporarily pushed aside, put aside while his hands had touched her as they were touching her now, making her momentarily forget unpaid bills, thoughtless words, careless actions.

"No, no, NO!" Claire was unaware that she had said the words aloud until she found herself released, the erotic pressure of David's body no longer pressing against her stomach, only the hard edges of the countertop forcing itself into her back. She reached out and placed a hand on the counter to steady herself, staring blindly up at a puzzled David.

"What is it, darling? What's the matter?"

But Claire couldn't respond, couldn't explain. She only knew she couldn't let this happen. It had been over four months since David had so much as touched her, since Christmas Eve when they'd both had a little too much to drink. She'd managed to keep things from getting out of hand then, and she'd promised herself she wouldn't let it happen again. And she'd prayed that if it did, then she wouldn't still feel this way. For God's sake, how long was it going to take! How long before they stopped having this need to...to *bond* every time they were so much as in the same room!

David was obviously not bothered by this intense sexual attraction he still felt for his ex-wife. Claire saw the smile hovering on his lips, saw the exultant look on his face. Damn him! She felt tears of frustration prick her eyes. He didn't care that she was never able to get close to another man because of him! He didn't care that she would probably spend the rest of her life a dried-up, lonely old lady because any other man's touch left her as cold and unmoved as a statue.

As if reading her thoughts, David said, "Truthfully, now, which would you rather have? Friendship with Lawrence, or this with me?" His voice was warm, husky, and he reached out to gather her to him again, sure of the answer.

His smugness, his sureness, was the final straw. "I *had* this with you—and I *left* you!" Claire said carefully, cruelly. "Does that answer your question?"

His hands fell away from her immediately, dropping limply to his sides. The hurt was naked in his eyes as he stared down at her, stunned by the truth of her words.

"Oh, David, I'm sorry!" Claire wailed, instantly contrite in the face of the pain she'd inflicted. "I didn't mean it like that! It's just—"

"No! No, you're right." He waved aside her apology, taking a deep breath and pulling himself up, straightening his shoulders. "You're perfectly right. You did leave. No denying that."

He took another deep breath while he ran long fingers through his blond hair. "Well, I guess that does answer my question, all right."

Claire was silent, feeling small and mean and cold, the cold vinyl floor chilling her bare feet as she stood helplessly in her kitchen in the middle of the night, being purposely hurtful.

The silence lengthened around them. Claire could hear the wind pushing and pulling at the house, prying at the loose shingles on the roof of the garage. David was staring at a place somewhere over her shoulder, seemingly lost in thought. Claire opened her mouth to speak, to say anything, anything to fill the painful, awkward void.

But David beat her to it, announcing suddenly, "If friends is what you want, then friends is what you'll get!"

"David—"

But he'd turned away from her and was slowly, tiredly walking back to the living room and picking up his coat. For once he looked each of his thirty-five years, Claire thought, all the boyish charm gone from his face as he pulled on his jacket. Claire could only

watch him silently, wishing she'd held her tongue—
wishing the truth weren't so painful.

She crossed over to stand beside him, resisting the
impulse to push aside the lock of hair that had fallen
across his forehead.

David raised his eyes to hers. "You're my wife,
Claire," he said slowly, intently. "You're my lover."
He paused, his blue eyes boring into hers as if trying
to see behind their physical reality, deeper, into her
soul. "And now you're going to be my friend." He
said the phrase tentatively, as if trying it on for size.

His gaze never left hers, but he lifted a hand to rub
briefly at a spot on his temple. "Okay." He exhaled,
blinking rapidly, forcing a smile to his lips. "Friends
it is. We'll give it a try."

Claire tried to find an answering smile, but it didn't
go much farther than her lips.

David's own smile became more genuine as he
watched her woebegone attempt. "Come on, friend."
He reached out a hand and took her small one in his.
"Walk me to the door. That sounds like a *friendly*
thing to do."

Claire held the door open for him, half hiding behind its bulk to protect her from the cold. Saying
good-night, she stood on her tiptoes to give him a
quick peck on the cheek.

David grimaced at the platonic gesture, but gamely
returned her goodbye and allowed her to shut the
door, leaving him standing on the doorstep. Turning,
he bounded up the stairs to his apartment, trying not
to think that it was his wife and his child that he'd left
below.

* * *

Claire clicked the dead bolt into place and stood leaning wearily against the door for a moment. Glancing at the clock, she knew she had better get to bed. She had clients scheduled every twenty minutes all day Monday and she would have to spend all of tomorrow preparing for them. She'd have to be up early to finish in time.

She walked over to the kitchen to flip off the light, but her hand paused on the switch. Who was she kidding? She knew she couldn't sleep. She'd just lay there, tossing and turning, thinking, going over the last half hour in her mind, replaying every scene until she drove herself crazy. She might as well wait until she was a little calmer before even attempting sleep.

She wandered over to the refrigerator and pulled open the door, surveying the interior. Oh, well, it looked as if she'd have to start a diet on Monday, she thought as she took out the pie tin holding one last piece of apple pie. She got a fork from the silverware drawer and, balancing the tin on her lap, curled up in the overstuffed chair in the corner of the living room to eat.

She still thought of it as David's chair. He'd always sat in it when they were married, claiming it had the best light since it was next to the large bay window at the front of the house. Personally Claire had always thought it was a cold spot, the window being of old-fashioned, single pane glass with the caulking around the casing cracked and missing in large chunks.

David had always been going to fix that, Claire thought, picking up the last crumbs of crust with her fork. He'd even gone so far as to buy the caulk. The tubes were still sitting out in the garage, as far as she knew—unopened, of course.

Claire leaned her head back in the chair, relaxing into its cushions. She hadn't really minded that carefree, careless side of David at first, she thought. It was just the way he was. She'd accepted it, knowing that creative, artistic people couldn't always be bothered with things such as drafty windows or plumbing or bills—or reality, she thought caustically.

Not that he hadn't worked, and worked hard, she admitted fairly. He'd always had a job, usually more than one at a time. But his first love, his career, was writing and so he never focused much energy into his outside jobs, never trying for promotions, never currying favor with his superiors. His jobs had been just—well, jobs. Nothing more. And they came and went depending on his mood at the time. Claire had provided some stability to their income with her job as an accountant with a large firm downtown. And they'd always gotten by, deliriously happy and in love.

But everything had changed, somehow, once they had Katy. Claire had quit her job to stay home with the baby and all of a sudden paychecks had taken on a new significance—or the lack of them had. She knew the change had mainly been within herself. She simply needed more stability, more security once she held that tiny, helpless little creature in her arms and realized that Katy was totally dependent on them.

She'd started worrying. She'd started nagging. She'd started having migraines. Claire found her hand moving automatically to the back of her head, rubbing at the spot where the pain had always been the worst, forcing her into bed for hours at a time.

The movement broke her reverie. All that was in the past, now, she told herself briskly. Over and done with. She stood up and took the empty pie tin into the kitchen. She was determined to move past David, to get on with her life. Surely this physical thing with him would have to lessen with time, she told herself, heading toward her bedroom.

As she pulled the covers up over her shoulders and settled the pillow more comfortably under her head, she tried to bring a picture of Lawrence into her mind. Solid, dependable, ever-kind Lawrence. She really did need to think about him and about his proposal. She really did. But as she quickly drifted off to sleep, Lawrence's brown eyes kept being overshadowed in her mind by ones that were blue—icy blue.

Two stories above, David was having no trouble at all keeping thoughts of Lawrence in his mind. From what Katy had been telling him, the old goat was getting serious. Not that he ever seemed to be anything *but* serious, David thought in disgust, twisting the cap off a bottle of beer and staring moodily out the window. How could Claire even consider tying herself down to a boring, middle-aged ... The man sold office supplies, for God's sake! David took a long swallow of beer, grimacing at the bitter taste.

I bet Lawrence is just one *hell* of a friend, he brooded, beginning to pace up and down. Friends! How did you go about being friends with someone when your heart and soul were already a part of theirs? When your body longed, *ached* to be part of theirs?

How was he ever supposed to be something as lukewarm and wishy-washy as *friends* with a woman like Claire. Didn't she see that they had so much more than that already? *Obviously not, Olson,* he told himself sarcastically, *since, as she so brutally pointed out, she left, remember?*

Of course Claire had been right to leave him, he thought morosely, stopping once again at the window. They'd always been broke and she'd had to work so hard. What kind of life was that for someone such as Claire? The swath of light on the grass in the backyard disappeared as Claire turned off her living-room light. He waited, watching at the window, until the light from her bedroom began to cast its glow in a different location on the grass.

Of course, things were different now, he reminded himself. Now he was rich. Now he— He paused in the middle of bringing the bottle of beer to his lips, frozen as the full impact of the thought hit him. He was practically rich! His mind began shouting at him in capital letters. He was a Number One Bestselling Author! He was a Book Of The Month Club Author!

Somehow, the full impact of it hadn't sunk in until this very moment. The past few months had been such a whirlwind. He'd been on three talk shows, countless interviews, constantly on the phone with his agent offering him new deals, new contracts. Stunned, he sank into a chair, the beer left forgotten on the windowsill.

Maybe Claire hadn't had time to really think about all of it, either, he told himself hopefully. Maybe she didn't realize that their life together now could be completely different than it was before. Barney, his agent, had just been talking to him today about movie rights, and what with the advance they'd offered him on his next book— Hell, he was more than practically rich! He was downright filthy rich!

A smile crossed his face and he looked eagerly at his watch. Was it too late to run down and see her now? Just as he jumped to his feet the backyard was blanketed in sudden darkness. Claire had gone to bed. *Oh well, never mind,* he thought happily. *First thing tomorrow I'll remind her that her husband—ex-husband, I mean—is a very wealthy man that can provide her with the kind of life old Lawrence-the-Liver-Spotted can only dream of!*

Chapter Three

It wasn't the alarm that woke her. Claire was sure of it. She'd been hitting the Snooze button every ten minutes since it had gone off at 6:00 a.m. She was sure it wasn't that horrible buzzing that had finally gotten through to her. Whatever it was, it was something horrible, though—and something wonderful, too.

She struggled to get her groggy mind to focus. Bacon. The smell of bacon frying. That was what was wonderful. That tantalizing, one-of-a-kind smell was what had woken her, she decided. She inhaled deeply, snuggling back into the warm blankets, thinking it had been at least two years since she'd had the pleasure of waking to such a delicious odor.

And that was what was horrible, too!

"Katy!" Claire had thrown back the blankets and was on her feet by the time the yell had escaped her mouth, jumping from the bed and running down the hall to the kitchen. The stove! Oh, my God!

She skidded around the corner, her mind frantically trying to remember if it was flour or baking powder you were supposed to throw on a grease fire. "Katy! You know better than to turn on—"

Claire stopped short in the middle of the kitchen floor. Katy was safely, if messily, standing on a chair pulled closely to the counter, up to her elbows in flour. Little white puffs of flour decorated the floor, the chair, the counter and Katy. David was standing behind her, belatedly trying to wrap one of Claire's aprons around her dusty pajamas, fumbling with the bow.

They had both half turned to stare at Claire, startled by her abrupt entrance. "We're making waffles, Momma," Katy told her, the first to recover. "From scratch," she added proudly, holding up her flour-covered hands as proof.

Claire moved to lean weakly against the refrigerator, trying to catch her breath and recover from the shock she had gotten at the idea of a five-year-old frying bacon. "We have waffles in the freezer," she informed the pair when she could talk.

"Those frozen, store-bought things?" David replied with a superior sniff. "You might just as well drop the box in the toaster for all the flavor they have. Waffles from a toaster!" He went back to tying Katy's bow. "The things I have to rescue this child from." He clucked his tongue.

Claire frowned at him. "Go home," she commanded, not in the mood for his banter. It was too early and she had too much work to do today. "Katy, you shouldn't let people into the house without asking me first."

"Daddy's not people," the child replied reasonably.

"Yeah, so there." David took a mug from the cupboard and filled it with fresh-brewed coffee. "Drink this," he ordered, carrying it over and handing it to her. "You look like you could use it."

Claire stuck her tongue out at him. "You two scared me to death. I thought Katy had decided to cook me breakfast in bed or something."

"Now *that's* an interesting idea." David wagged his eyebrows insinuatingly.

But Claire ignored him. "I meant it," she said, making little shooing motions with her fingers. "Go back upstairs and take all this food with you. I've got a load of work to do today and I won't be able to concentrate if I stuff myself on waffles."

"With fresh strawberries and whipped cream," he said, temptingly. "Eggs over easy with the edges crunchy, just like you like them. And bacon with the fat barely turning brown so it's still sort of chewy—"

"Stop it!" she groaned. She hated him. Her diet hated him.

This time it was he who ignored her. He was concentrating on gently prying golden waffles from the waffle iron—a contraption he must have brought with him because Claire most certainly didn't own such a thing.

After a moment he looked over his shoulder at her, a barely suppressed grin on his face. "You know,

Claire, you're not being very gracious about this," he admonished. "I'm just trying to be *friendly.*"

She groaned again, louder this time, wishing she'd never mentioned the word last night.

"Breakfast is almost ready," he told her, piling the waffles on a nearby plate. "You better go get dressed. I've already seen you in that outfit."

And for just a moment, as he stood there grinning at her, the years fell away and Claire remembered. Remembered other mornings, and other breakfasts. And she couldn't help smiling in return. Suddenly she didn't feel so tired or so grumpy anymore. What the hell. What were a few more calories, anyway.

Meekly she turned and retraced her steps back to her bedroom. She peeled off the T-shirt and replaced it with a hot-pink sweatshirt. Then she tugged on a pair of faded jeans and laced up her white, high-top tennis shoes. Pulling her hair back into a ponytail and tying it with a pink ribbon, she felt ready to face any-thing—a huge breakfast, a too-charming ex-husband, a briefcase full of work.

But as the three of them sat at the table—eating, talking, teasing each other—Claire tried not to think how comfortable, how natural, it seemed to be to-gether this way again. And she wished David wouldn't look as if he were thinking the very same thing. He was watching the two of them demolish his cooking with the satisfied air of a man who knows he's truly appre-ciated—the air of a man who's come home.

Seeming to read her mind, David said, "We've got to do this more often. The women I've been cooking for lately always seem to be on diets. It's damned depressing." He shook his head sadly. "Hey, I've got an idea!" he said, brightening. "Why don't we head for the park and do some ice skating this morning! The pond should still be frozen for another week or so—it'd be perfect!"

Katy had started to bounce in her chair excitedly but Claire was shaking her head before he'd even finished. "Come on," he coaxed. "We could all use the exercise after this breakfast. Your work can wait till this afternoon, can't it?"

"It can wait?" Claire stared at him in amazement. "For God's sake, David, haven't you looked at a calendar lately?" Obviously not, she realized, seeing his blank look. "Don't you know what today is?"

"Sunday." He stabbed the last bite of waffle on his nearly empty plate. "So what?"

"I mean the date."

"April 12," David replied, still puzzled.

Claire rolled her eyes in exasperation. "Do words like accountant—IRS—*taxes* mean anything to you? I'm a C.P.A., David, remember? My life revolves around—"

"April 15!" he said, waving his fork triumphantly as he finally got her point. "Sorry. I forgot about it being tax time and all that."

"Which reminds me," she said, pushing away her plate and reaching for her coffee cup. "Did you get together your royalty statements and all your expense receipts like I asked you to? I'm not going to spend all Wednesday evening doing your taxes like I did last year," she warned. "No more mad dashes to the post office at 11:59! I've got other clients to take care of. *Paying* clients, I might add."

"Do you need some money?" David asked, immediately contrite. He stood up and reached into his front pants pocket, digging around. "I paid last month's child support, didn't I? I know I paid the rent—I think." He pulled out a wad of bills, and Claire could see several hundred-dollar bills mixed carelessly in with a bunch of ones.

She shook her head in exasperation. She knew it was disorganization, not lack of money, that made him so lackadaisical in his payments. "No, I don't need money," she told him. "You know I make more than you do. Or at least I did," she amended, "before your book."

David looked up. This was just the opportunity he'd been waiting for! A chance to approach her about the revelation he'd had last night.

"Claire, I wanted to talk to you about that—about money, I mean." He laid two hundred-dollar bills on the table and stuffed the rest haphazardly back into his pocket.

"What about it?" she asked, pushing back her chair and standing up. She began to clear the table, pointedly ignoring the money he'd laid there. After his book sold, he had immediately doubled both his child support payments and his rent. She didn't need any more of his money, in spite of the way she liked to dig him about it.

"Well, about how much of it I have, for one thing," he replied. "Do you know how much money I have!"

"I know exactly how much money you have," she told him matter-of-factly, carrying a stack of dishes to the sink. "I'm your accountant, remember? And if you want to give any more of it away to those worthless friends of yours, that's just too bad! I've tied up what's left of your last royalty check in a long-term certificate." She started to rinse the plates under a stream of warm water.

"You've got the bulk of your money in T-bills at a fairly decent interest rate," Claire began to explain. "But I've been thinking of maybe investing in some municipal bonds. They're safe and there's the tax advantage—" She broke off and turned to look at him suspiciously. "Why the sudden interest in your money?"

"I didn't mean how it was invested," David said with an exasperated sigh, wishing Claire didn't take everything to do with money so *literally*. "I know you're taking care of all that. I assume Katy will inherit handsomely when I die."

"Are you going to die, Daddy?" Katy piped up, giving him a worried look before she bent her head to start licking the whipped cream off her plate.

"Never, sweetheart," David assured her, pulling the plate out from underneath her protruding tongue. "Why don't you go play? I want to talk to your mother about grown-up things for a minute."

Katy looked from one adult to the other, considering. "Okay, I'll go. But there'll be no fighting, understand!" she warned with a wag of her finger. "Seems like I can't leave you two alone for a minute."

Claire had to struggle to suppress a smile. "You're getting to be a smart-mouthed little thing lately, young lady!" she said, trying to look stern.

Katy blinked up at her mother solemnly. "I need a father's stabilizing influence, I guess."

"Stabilizing! Hah!" Claire knew Katy hadn't come up with that phrase on her own. And the way David had quickly turned his back to smother a laugh confirmed where she had probably heard it. "Scram, kiddo," Claire ordered, taking a quick wipe at the child's sticky face with the dishrag. "And if you're going to watch TV, try to make it something a little bit educational, okay?"

Katy skipped from the room, and Claire could soon hear the muted sounds of the television.

"What I meant was—" David began again, trying to get the conversation back on track. "What I meant was, do you realize how much money I have to *spend?*"

"A lot," Claire said. "By the way, have they offered you an advance on your next book?"

David couldn't resist taking the opportunity to tease her a little. She was so damned materialistic about the work of writing, something he had always considered a work of *art*. "I'm not sure there's going to be another book," he announced serenely, reaching around her to grab the last piece of bacon off a plate just as she was about to scrape it down the disposal. "I only had one story to tell, and I told it."

"David!" Claire was shocked to the core, her hands frozen in midair. "You can't be serious! You have entire *files* full of plots and characters and—"

"Do you remember *To Kill a Mockingbird?*" he interrupted. "That was Harper Lee's first book—won a Pulitzer prize, by the way—but it was also her last book."

"*The Green of Spring* was one of the best murder mysteries I've ever read, but it wasn't exactly Pulitzer prize winning material, and you know it!" Claire chided. "Besides, that's not the point! You're a hot item right now. People will buy any book you write. You—"

She was so earnest David couldn't help laughing out loud. "Settle down, Claire," he said. "I'm just teasing you. In fact, I'm close to halfway finished with the next adventure of our favorite detective." He had to duck quickly to avoid the wet dishrag she threw at him, darting out to grab it before it landed in the bowl of waffle batter.

"*And* they're in the process of cutting me a check for an enormous sum of money to encourage me to finish it," he added, coming to stand beside her. As he dropped the rag back into the basin of soapy water she was filling, he named a figure that had Claire's eyes widening in shock.

"You're kidding!" she gasped.

"Pretty impressive, huh?" David reached out to turn off the faucet before it spilled bubbles over the top of the sink. "So, that's what I wanted to talk to you about. About how we're going to spend such a fortune." He poured them both a fresh cup of coffee and led Claire over to the table. The dishes could wait.

"What's this *we* business," Claire protested, sitting in the chair he pulled out for her. "Spending your money has nothing to do with me."

"You're missing the point here, Claire," David sighed. "We're talking about money! Money! I have it, now."

"So?"

"So wasn't that what we were always fighting over when we were married?"

"It did tend to be a recurring theme," Claire admitted, taking a sip of coffee.

"So if lack of money was the problem with our marriage, now that it's not a problem anymore, then—"

Immediately Claire understood what he was driving at. She set her cup down on the table with a clatter. "Now just one minute!" She held up her hand to stop him from going any further, shaking her head vehemently. "Money was not *the* problem with our marriage," she declared. "It was just one of the *many* problems!"

"But think how different it could be now!" David was leaning toward her, elbows on the table, excitement in his voice. "We could travel—Europe, the Orient. We could finally fix up the house—hell, we could sell the house and move to... to anywhere! Hawaii! You always wanted to see where your great-grandmother was born! We could buy a winter house in Hawaii! We could—"

"*That* was the problem," Claire interrupted dryly.

"What?" He didn't understand, still caught up in his plans.

"Selling the house. Moving. Dreams, schemes, plans—" Claire shrugged. "To you, those things are adventure—to me, they're nothing but lack of security." In spite of herself, she found her voice falling into the old, singsong criticizing pattern as she continued. "Always wondering when you were going to come up with another harebrained scheme to blow the last of our savings on. Worrying when you were going to get tired of your job and quit—with no thought of how we were going to buy groceries if you did! It was never lack of money that we were really fighting about. It was lack of *security!* For me, for Katy, for our future."

"I wasn't that bad, was I, Claire?" David asked quietly, when she paused to draw breath. "We always managed to get by. I always provided for us."

"Of course you did! I'm not trying to denigrate those years together, it's just—"

"And I suppose Lawrence can provide you with this precious *security,* then?" he interrupted with undisguised sarcasm.

"*I* can provide it for me," Claire insisted, green eyes beginning to flash. "Once I don't have to worry about *your* next move!" She gave an impatient shake of her head. She wasn't trying to hurt him—to place blame. They hadn't talked this way in a long time and she didn't want it to end in a shouting match. It was important to make him understand.

Choosing her words carefully, she said, "I'm not talking about only monetary security. There's such a thing as *emotional* security."

"Meaning what?" David demanded.

She hesitated, searching for an example. "Like that kayaking trip of yours to Alaska! What about that? It wasn't so much that you took every last dime we had to pay for it, but you left me with a six-week-old baby and took off to iceberg heaven with never a *thought* that something might happen to you. That I might be left widowed, struggling to care for the two of us." She pointed an accusing finger at him. "You could have gotten yourself killed and we wouldn't have known for weeks! You deliberately put yourself in a dangerous situation with no concern for anyone but yourself!"

David leaned back in his chair impatiently. "Oh, Claire, it was perfectly safe! It was a once in a lifetime opportunity and Joe was an experienced guide. Hell, that bear never really got that close at all!"

"Bear! What bear?"

"One good whack on the nose and he took right off."

"What bear?" Claire repeated.

"I didn't tell you about that?" David asked, suddenly looking sheepish. "Well, never mind." He waved his hand dismissingly. "I see your point. As always, you're perfectly right." His face lost its hardness and he dropped his defensive posture. He smiled at her, his voice once again persuasive. "But now you'd *have* security, don't you see?" he pleaded. "All kinds of security! You'd have financial security, you'd have trust funds for our old age, you'd have me sitting at home doing nothing more dangerous than getting zapped with radiation from my word processor!"

But Claire was shaking her head. He still didn't understand.

"Think of Katy!" he told her, feeling desperate now. "How can you say you don't want more for Katy?"

"You're already spoiling her rotten!" Claire exclaimed. "I've set you up a trust for her so she'll always be provided for. *Well* provided for. She doesn't need to live like a spoiled little rich kid now."

David scraped back his chair and stood up, his patience gone. He glared down at her. "You are being stubborn and vindictive and—"

Claire stood to face him. "And you're trying to *buy* back a marriage!" Their voices had risen to near shouting level by now.

"At least—"

"I said no fighting!" Katy's worried voice came through to them from the living room. "You promised!"

They both looked guiltily at each other. "All right, sweetheart, we're sorry," David called to the child. He took a deep breath, letting it out as he ran his hands through his blond hair, trying to calm himself.

"I'm sorry, Claire. I just thought—I just thought that maybe now, with the book and the money and all, that things could be different."

Claire wanted to respond with all her heart. How could she turn her back on him—but how could she not? "It's not *things* I want to be different, David. It's *us* I want to be different."

"Yeah, I remember," he said glumly. "Friends. We're supposed to be friends." His voice gave the word a depressing ring.

"Your friendship would mean more to me than your money."

And she meant it. David could see that in her eyes, could hear the sincerity in her voice. He was a very confused man.

They finished cleaning the kitchen, then David gathered up his waffle iron and his daughter and left Claire alone for the day to concentrate on her clients' tax returns. She worked diligently for the next two hours, her adding machine spewing great long coils of tape out over the edge of the table to curl on the floor by her feet. The morning sun moved slowly across the floor as she worked, highlighting tiles strip by strip, until it finally reached the spot where she sat, climbing the table legs to spread its golden light across the forms she was hunched over.

The change in light broke Claire's concentration. She glanced up, her gaze automatically going to the window. The clouds of last night were clearing rapidly, the still-weak sun doing its best to melt snow that had outstayed its welcome on the north side of the yard. Claire stood up and stretched, kicking aside the tangle of adding machine tape and eyeing it with disfavor. It would get a lot longer before she was through for the day, she knew. Her legs felt stiff from sitting. She leaned over and touched her toes, then reached her hands high overhead, leaning from one side to another, trying to get her circulation started again.

Sighing, she forced herself to sit back down. She took a sip of coffee, long-cold, fiddled with the lead in her pencil and straightened a stack of papers. Then, impulsively, she threw down the pencil and stood up. She was going for a walk. Who knew how long the sunshine might last? Slipping into her jacket, she grabbed her house keys and headed for the door. She pulled it shut behind her and locked it with a click.

A similar click sounded above her head. Claire looked up at the door to the second floor apartment she'd recently rented to a retired air force captain and his wife. It was the wife who had just pulled her own key out of the lock and was starting down the stairs toward her. Claire couldn't help staring as the woman approached.

Naomi Maxwell was a woman in her early fifties with the body of a woman fifteen years younger. She was obviously dressed for jogging in a body-hugging, one piece suit of shiny neon purple. A gray flannel sweatshirt with the sleeves torn off in the latest fashion was layered over the suit, cropped to hang just below her firm bust. A lime-green sweatband circled her head, making a rather startling contrast to hair a shade of red that proudly proclaimed it came from a bottle. Her face was carefully made up, even for a Sunday morning run, and as she reached up to clasp the headphones of her cassette player around her neck, Claire noticed that her long fingernails sported a bright coat of pink polish.

"Hello, Mrs. Maxwell," Claire greeted her new tenant politely.

"Oh, call me Naomi, for heaven's sake," the woman replied, bounding down the remainder of the stairs to join Claire. "Mrs. Maxwell is the Captain's mother. Even he calls her that, the old battle-ax."

Claire laughed. "Naomi," she repeated. "This sunshine is too good to waste, isn't it? I'm more than ready for spring this year."

"I'll say," Naomi agreed. "Old retired people like the Captain and me should be in Florida, not Minnesota." She began to jog in place, bouncing lightly on her toes, warming up before starting off. "Care to join me for a little run?"

Claire laughed again. Last weekend, driving home from the mall, she'd passed Naomi at least four miles from the apartment, running with a professional-looking stride and appearing not the least bit winded. Little run!

"No, thanks." She shook her head emphatically. "I'm more the 'brisk walk' type myself."

"Nothing wrong with a little brisk walking," Naomi replied good-naturedly. "Mind if I tag along for a mile or so? It will be a good, slow warm-up. I pulled a hamstring a while back and it's still a little sore."

Claire agreed readily enough and the two started down the sidewalk. Claire gave the newcomer a brief introduction to some of their neighbors' homes, attaching names and interesting pieces of gossip to each, and they enjoyed trying to spot the first signs of spring in the carefully tended flower beds of the old houses.

"How are you liking the area?" she asked Naomi, pausing to point out a crocus, tucked away underneath a shaggy lilac bush. "Any problems with the apartment? Anything I can do to make you more comfortable?"

"Oh, we've settled in just fine," Naomi assured her. "And we love the neighborhood. It's so peaceful. Not overrun with dogs and kids—yet." She eyed the swing set and chain-link dog run in the yard of one of the new, younger additions to the neighborhood.

"I hope Katy hasn't been making too much noise," Claire said, automatically feeling guilty. "I'm afraid these old houses aren't soundproofed very well."

"Not to worry. Your little girl is as sweet as can be. She's already come visiting a couple of times." Naomi stopped at a corner and knelt down to retie her shoelace. Her voice was casual as she added, "And the man who lives upstairs, David Olson, he's stopped by, too." She looked up at Claire innocently. "He seems very nice. Charming, in fact."

Claire nodded. "Yes, he is."

"He and the Captain really hit it off." She straightened up and they resumed walking, but Claire could see the woman looking at her out of the corner of her eye—considering. "So, he writes, does he?" she said, after they'd gone a few more yards.

Claire nodded again. "Yes, he does."

"I've never met a famous writer before. I saw him on one of those morning talk shows a couple weeks ago. He was great," Naomi said admiringly. "He had the audience practically eating out of his hand."

"Yes, he did," Claire agreed. She'd seen the same show.

They walked along quietly for a while but Claire could see Naomi's curious looks and knew she was itching to find the answers to some rather personal questions. Such as why her landlady and her fellow tenant had the same last name. And why Katy's eyes had the same exotic tilt as Claire's but were the ice-blue color of David's? And why the little girl ran back and forth between the two apartments, equally at home in both places?

Finally Naomi could stand it no longer. "You know, one of the privileges of age is being able to ask prying questions that are absolutely none of your business," she said bluntly. "And I was wondering—"

Claire laughed. "We're divorced."

"Ahh." Naomi nodded with satisfaction, red curls bobbing. "That explains it! I mean, I've heard of husband and wives having separate bedrooms, but separate apartments? Of course, I thought maybe being an artistic type he might need a lot of personal space but, still, it seemed curious."

"It just so happened that the upstairs apartment was between tenants the day I kicked David out," Claire explained, pausing to turn up the collar of her coat against the breeze that had just started up. "I needed the income and he needed the cheap rent—and we both wanted him to be near Katy. It was supposed to be a temporary arrangement till he found something better—but it's been almost two years now and it's really worked fairly well. Of course, now that his book is doing so well, he'll probably want to move into something fancier." Claire found herself frowning even as she said the words. She'd never considered that before. David could afford the fanciest penthouse in Minneapolis—forget Minneapolis! The fanciest penthouse anywhere! Maybe he'd decide to move to New York, closer to his agent and editor. Maybe—

"Excuse me?" She realized she hadn't been paying attention to Naomi's conversation.

"I was just saying there aren't many divorced couples who could live so close to each other—happily, that is."

"Hah! David just pretends we're still married," Claire responded wryly. "And I think Katy probably does, too. You know, maybe it will be a good thing if he does move," she mused aloud. "Maybe then we can finally make a clean break—really make an effort to start new lives—" She stopped, seeing that once again Naomi was regarding her strangely. She supposed she *had* made their relationship sound rather bizarre.

"Well, I think it's nice that you two can be friends," Naomi said, letting Claire's remarks pass without comment.

Friends! Sure! If we could be friends, we'd still be married, Claire thought to herself sarcastically. Or maybe we can only be friends if we're divorced. She'd have to think about that one. She forced her attention back to Naomi's words.

"You know, David sort of reminds me of an old boyfriend of mine. Thomas— Hmm, Thomas somebody." She waved a pink tipped hand dismissingly. "The man could charm the socks right off you. Gorgeous, witty, smooth-talking. All the girls were crazy about him. But then the Captain came along." An affectionate smile touched her lips. "Boring old Captain whose line was about as smooth as sandpaper. And, you know, I never gave that Thomas what's his name another thought."

"Men like that Thomas are fascinating, all right, no denying that—but they're sort of like desserts, don't you think?" She gave Claire a penetrating look. "You might crave them, you might positively drool over them, but they don't really fill you up. If you had to eat dessert three meals a day, day after day, all of a sudden boring old meat and potatoes would look pretty good. You know what I mean?"

Claire voiced her agreement, but inwardly she smiled, thinking how David would laugh when she told him Naomi had insinuated he was like dessert. But then the smile faded and she sobered. No. She wouldn't tell him after all. That would only give him an opening—a chance to remind her of her notorious sweet tooth.

Chapter Four

It was eight o'clock by the time Claire finally escorted her last client to the door. Pushing it shut with a thankful sigh, she wearily made her way back to her desk and turned off the power to her adding machine for the first time since before sunrise that morning. She spent a few minutes straightening up the clutter of papers covering the desktop, then she pushed in her chair and clicked off the lamp—only to immediately click it back on again.

Claire reached out, and with a purposeful twist of her wrist, ripped off the top page of her open desk calendar. She crumpled April 15 into a tight little ball and neatly tossed it into the overflowing wastebasket. Another tax year survived.

Once again Claire pulled the chain on the lamp, darkening the spare bedroom she used for an office.

It was time to get Katy. Poor darling. She'd hardly spent a minute with her the last three days. Claire quickly left her apartment and made her way upstairs. Thank God she had an ex-husband living under the same roof, she told herself distractedly. But then a frown wrinkled her brow as she realized the significance of her thought.

David had been picking up his daughter from kindergarten and keeping her until Claire finished work for the day. And, declaring that Katy needed something more nutritious than cereal for supper, he'd taken to fixing them all a nighttime meal, too. Claire's frown deepened. She'd been so busy lately, she hadn't let herself dwell on just how "family" they'd been these past few days. But now it was time to put a stop to it, she decided. Times such as this only encouraged David with his ridiculous reconciliation scheme.

She mentally vowed to make an effort to be sure life got back to normal again. Now that tax season was behind her, she'd see that they each retreated to their own apartments once more—where they belonged.

Reaching the third floor, Claire pushed open David's door without knocking—a habit she'd somehow gotten into lately. David was standing at the stove, stirring something in a steaming pot, and he glanced over at her as she entered.

No, this would never do, Claire thought to herself grimly when she saw the look on David's face as he smiled a greeting. He was looking too damn comfortable! David was looking all too much like a man who had things going exactly according to plan. A plan Claire wanted no part of!

"Spaghetti will be ready in a second," he told her. "I'm just cooking some fresh pasta." He started to add the long strands of spaghetti to the pot a few pieces at a time, slowly, waiting for the water to come back to a boil. She'd read somewhere you were supposed to do it that way—not dump it in in one big clump as she usually did.

"Katy?" Claire asked, glancing around for her daughter. She pulled out a chair and seated herself at the table, noticing that it was only set for two.

"Out like a light," David told her. "She tried so hard to stay awake, but after I fed her and gave her a bath she just couldn't make it another minute. How about we let her stay the night?"

Claire nodded her agreement, realizing with a pang that she hadn't so much as seen her daughter since early morning. Yes, it was definitely time to get their old routine back again. They could survive without David's cooking.

Although the smell of that spaghetti sauce was certainly tantalizing, she had to admit, sniffing appreciatively when David lifted the lid to give the sauce a quick stir, letting an aromatic burst fill the kitchen. Appearing satisfied, he replaced the lid and moved to pick up a bottle of wine waiting on the counter. With efficient movements, he pried out the cork and poured them each a glass.

Claire gratefully reached out to take hers. She seldom drank alcohol, but tonight a glass of wine, sparkling a deep rich red, somehow seemed in order.

"To the IRS," David proclaimed solemnly, raising his glass in her direction for a toast.

"Here, here," Claire agreed, taking a sip. Hmm, perfect, she thought, savoring the wine's slightly sweet bouquet. She knew absolutely nothing about wine—except that old was supposed to be good—but David never failed to produce something special. She took another swallow, then sat the wineglass down and scooted her chair closer to the table, leaning forward on her elbows. "I'm starving," she announced. "When does the timer ding?"

"Ding? My dear Claire," David said with a resigned shake of his head, "pasta is not cooked to the ding of a timer. Pasta is cooked *al dente*—to the teeth!" He went to the stove and picked up a fork, then fished through the boiling water until he caught a strand of spaghetti. Breaking off a piece with his fingers, he popped it into his mouth, making a show of feeling its texture tentatively with tongue and teeth. "Four minutes," he proclaimed pompously.

"*You* are a showoff," Claire told him severely.

"Agreed," he said, laying down the fork with a flourish. "And *you* are a rotten cook."

"Agreed," she echoed, smiling and feeling some of the tiredness leave her. And she felt even better a half hour later, her stomach pleasantly full of spaghetti and her head pleasantly feeling the effects of a second glass of wine.

David, noticing her work-day tension easing away, broke the companionable silence they'd shared for most of the meal. "So, where do you want to go tomorrow night to celebrate?" he asked.

"The only way I want to celebrate getting through tax season is with a long bath and an early bed."

"That wasn't exactly what I wanted to celebrate." David picked up the nearly empty bottle of wine and made to refill her glass, but Claire waved him away, giving him a puzzled look.

"I meant celebrating our anniversary," he explained, seeing the look.

"Our anniversary was in September," she reminded him.

"I'm talking about our *other* anniversary." When Claire's face still remained blank, he continued patiently, "The anniversary of our divorce. You kicked me out two years ago tomorrow, if you'll remember."

"Oh, I remember, all right! It's not like I make a habit of it."

"Exactly! I thought we should celebrate such a momentous occasion."

"Yuck." Claire's voice echoed the look of distaste on her face. "That's a morbid idea. People don't celebrate divorces."

"Well, maybe celebrate isn't exactly the right word," David conceded. "Maybe I mean pay tribute to...acknowledge...commemorate... You want me to find my thesaurus?"

"I get the idea," Claire said dryly. "And I think it's a silly idea."

"That's because you're tired," he informed her, his enthusiasm not diminished by her lack of it. "But when you wake up in the morning—after sleeping in late, wallowing in bed—you'll find yourself looking forward to a chance to get all fancied up and spend an evening dining and dancing with me."

"Oh, I will, will I?"

"Yup, especially after I mention I had in mind something special—like dinner at The Garden."

Claire's eyes widened. She couldn't help but be impressed with the name of the most expensive, trendiest restaurant in the city. "My, my! So you want to spend an evening mingling with the rich and famous, do you?"

"I want to spend an evening mingling with you," David told her. "Remember how well we used to mingle?" He jumped to his feet and, with a smooth motion, pulled her up from her chair and into his arms, twirling her in an intricate pattern of dance steps across the kitchen floor.

Humming an exuberant mixture of rumba and cha-cha, he ended with a flourish close to the refrigerator, leaning her backward over his arm until her long hair was brushing the floor. He brought his face down to within inches of her own. "Tah-dah!" he exclaimed softly, providing his own finale. "Damn, I forgot how good we were!"

Claire couldn't stop the laughter that bubbled up from inside her. David could always make her feel so good! She might curse his lighthearted outlook toward life when the faucet dripped or the spark plugs needed cleaning, but when it came to dancing across kitchen floors and making her feel as if she were the sexiest woman alive—damn, she'd forgotten how good he was!

And now, with his blue eyes laughing into hers, his body fitting familiarly, intimately, over hers, almost lying on top of her as he held her bent over his arm—how could she keep from melting? And he was looking so sexy—barefooted, in thigh-hugging jeans with a spaghetti-sauce-stained dish towel tucked into his back pocket, and a V-necked sweater, its sleeves pushed carelessly up to reveal his strong forearms.

Claire felt her heart begin to quicken its beat and her breathing become no more than a light flutter of air. The blood was beginning to pound in her ears, and she knew it wasn't all due to her upside-down position.

"Let me up!" she demanded, her helpless giggles quieting as she struggled to right herself and regain her mental as well as physical equilibrium. "All the blood's rushing to my head!"

"Not until you promise," David told her firmly, holding her down with ease despite her efforts.

"Okay, okay, we'll have dinner."

"Great!" He started to pull her up. "I bet Naomi would love to watch Katy for us. She said she would anytime."

"Oh!" Claire wailed as she suddenly remembered the practicalities of an evening out. "David, I can't be leaving Katy at a sitter's again! I've hardly seen her all week. I— David!" she squealed as she felt herself being pushed backward over his arm once more, helplessly watching the world invert. She flailed her arms clutching him around the neck, trying to keep her balance.

"You haven't been leaving Katy at a sitter—you've been leaving her with her father," David pointed out reasonably. "And besides, you promised. Right?" He waited for her answer. "You're starting to get all red faced again," he warned.

"All right, you brute," Claire laughed. "I did promise. I'll ask Naomi to watch Katy."

Effortlessly David lifted her back to her feet, pulling her against him in the process since her arms were still locked around his neck. They stood that way for a moment, silently, the smile fading from her lips and his, their gazes locked. Claire had to fight to keep from closing her eyes against the flood of feelings that swelled over her as her treacherous body instinctively molded itself against him in ways that had been so natural for so many years. Summoning all of her strength, she forced herself to stiffen, sucking in her breath, drawing back to put a mere fraction of an inch between them. She unclasped her hands from around his neck and allowed them to fall to her side.

A slight smile touched David's mouth once again, and his eyes mocked her efforts to withdraw, to try to distance herself from him. He had felt her tremble. He knew.

Without a word he raised her unresisting arms, repositioning her left hand back behind his neck and keeping her right hand tightly in his own. His breath fanned the hair on her forehead as he began humming a tune. His feet started moving again and the hand he placed on her hip forced her body to move with his.

Claire closed her eyes and let her head fall forward to tuck under his chin. She sighed.

And for the next half hour she danced with her ex-husband in his kitchen. Barefoot. Without music. He nostalgically remembering and she desperately trying to forget.

* * *

The next morning Claire got Katy onto the school bus, then went upstairs to visit the Maxwells. Naomi greeted her warmly and invited her in for coffee.

"We haven't seen much of you, lately," Naomi said, filling two mugs and taking them to the kitchen table. "Sam, look who's here," she called into the living room where her husband was seated at a large table, papers and books spread out around him. Hearing his name, the Captain looked up and gave Claire a distracted nod before bending over the yellow legal pad he was writing in.

Naomi rolled her eyes. "That game! He's spent all morning working on some new idea that came to him in the middle of the night. Something about dice, I think."

Claire knew Captain Maxwell had developed a complicated board game involving military strategy and little pewter figures and that he was using his recent retirement to fine-tune the war game before he tried to market it.

"I've been pretty busy with work, myself," Claire said, explaining her absence. "But I'm taking today off—giving myself a little vacation."

"How nice! And are you doing anything special with your holiday?"

"As a matter of fact, that's why I stopped by," Claire told her. "David and I wanted to go out to dinner tonight and we were wondering if you might be able to watch Katy for us?"

"Of course we could," Naomi agreed readily. "It will be perfect, since our grandchildren are coming over this evening, too!"

"Are you sure it won't be too much trouble?" Claire could just imagine what havoc a houseful of children could wreak on the Captain's papers.

"Heaven's no," Naomi assured her. "In fact, it will make it easier. It will give them someone new to play with. Won't it, dear?" she added, raising her voice to project into the other room.

The Captain nodded again, not bothering to look up this time.

Claire gave Naomi her heartfelt thanks. Trying to find someone besides her grandparents to watch Katy was a source of never ending frustration. "I didn't know you had family nearby," she said to Naomi, settling down for a chat.

The older woman pointed to a group of pictures hanging on the opposite wall. "Our daughter lives in St. Paul," she said. "When Sam retired last year we thought it would be nice to be near her, so we decided to come up here and give a Minnesota winter a trial run—see if we could emerge in the spring with our sanity intact. Isn't that right, dear?"

Claire could see the Captain's silver-haired head bobbing up and down on cue, although she'd bet his wife's words hadn't penetrated his concentration at all. Claire knew she'd heard the man speak at some time or another, but now that she thought about it, she couldn't recall exactly when that might have been.

But Naomi seemed satisfied with his response. She took a sip of coffee and continued, "And now it's

April and we're still here—although there was a spell there in February when I spent an awful lot of time leafing through condo brochures from Phoenix and Miami.''

Claire smiled in sympathy. February was a short but dreary month in Minnesota. "So you think you might stay, then?"

Naomi grimaced. "The vote's still out. We don't want to be too hasty. Financially we're fortunate enough to be able to pick pretty much anyplace we want. We've been lucky that way—a lot of our friends are finding retirement a nightmare.''

"Retirement." Claire made the word a worried sigh. "With interest rates fluctuating the way they are—it makes it impossible to plan!"

Naomi's well-plucked eyebrows raised in surprise at the vehemency of the younger woman's tone. "Well, you still have a while before you need to be concerned with retirement," she said with a smile.

But Claire shook her head, her face serious. "It's never too early to start saving for something like that. I've got a little nest egg put away now and as long as interest rates stay at least seven percent I should be able to retire in thirty-seven years and be fairly comfortable—especially with the equity in the house.'' Claire frowned and gave her coffee a distracted stir. "Depending on inflation, of course. And if the real estate market holds.''

She looked up from her coffee cup to see Naomi staring at her oddly. "What?" Claire asked, wondering what she'd said that was unusual. "What is it?"

"How old are you, anyway?"

"Twenty-eight."

"And you've been saving for your retirement—"

"Since I was twenty-one," Claire supplied promptly.

Silence followed this disclosure, while Naomi continued to discomfit her with her stare.

Then, abruptly, Naomi asked, "What are you wearing tonight? To dinner, I mean."

Claire blinked in surprise, not following the sudden change in topic. "I don't know—I haven't really thought about it." She shrugged her shoulders. "I guess, well, I have a black dress that I usually wear for things like this."

"Has David seen you in it?"

Claire nodded.

"That settles it then," Naomi announced briskly, rising from her chair. "Come on. We're going shopping."

"Now? Oh, no. No, I couldn't possibly—"

"I thought you had the day off?" Naomi demanded.

"I do, but—"

"Well, then, let's go buy you something dazzling."

But Claire was shaking her head. "I can't afford a new dress," she protested. "I can't *possibly* afford a new dress, I mean I—" She stuttered to a close, suddenly aware how automatically her negative words had come out. Actually she could afford a new dress, she thought in surprise. Since Katy had started school she'd been able to take on more clients. In fact, her client list had grown to almost more than she could handle alone.

The house didn't need any major repairs, the car was running fine... Why not a new dress? The words "I can't afford it" had been said, and been true, so many times in the past that now they came to her lips of their own accord—more out of habit than anything else.

Claire realized she was sitting there openmouthed, Naomi standing above her expectantly. "Maybe you're right," she said, a pleased smile brightening her face. "A new dress sounds like a great idea!"

"Well, don't just sit there! Go get your purse and your credit cards and let's hit the mall!"

Naomi waved her young guest out the door, then refilled her coffee cup and took it into the living room to stand next to her husband.

"Sam, did you hear that?" she demanded. But she didn't pause for a response. She continued, "That poor child has got the next thirty-seven years of her life all mapped out—or at least she thinks she does! Can you believe it? Goodness, she'll make herself old before her time trying to organize and plan everything like that. I bet she's never done anything spontaneous in her life!"

Naomi's long pink nails tapped on the ceramic coffee mug while she considered for a moment. "That young lady needs someone to help loosen her up," she decided with a firm nod of her red curls. "Yes, indeed." She turned on her heel and started to walk back to the kitchen, still murmuring to herself. "And a very peculiar relationship she has with her husband, too, if I say so myself. What Claire needs..."

Captain Sam Maxwell half turned in his chair, looking after his wife. He raised a detaining hand and his mouth opened to speak. But upon seeing the determined set of his wife's back, he wisely pressed his lips together and returned to his papers.

Later that evening, Claire found herself silently blessing her neighbor as she stood in front of the mirror in her new dress, eyeing her reflection with a pleasure tinged with just a touch of vain excitement. She looked good! And it was all thanks to Naomi.

Naomi had been the one who had kept steering her away from the reduced price racks in the back of the store where she was used to shopping. Naomi was the one who had firmly slapped her hand away each time Claire had tried to pull up the sleeve of a dress to look at the price tag.

And the result was dynamite, Claire had to admit as she turned, craning her neck over her shoulder to get a better look at the daring design of the back of the dress. The emerald-green silk sheath had a high mandarin collar and long, tight sleeves but the back was open almost to her waist, exposing a rather breathtaking amount of bare skin. Untwisting herself, Claire took a few exaggeratedly slinky, hip swinging steps toward the mirror, watching the slits along each side of the knee-length skirt widen provocatively. Oh, my!

Claire's grin of delight was at odds with the sophisticated sensuality of the dress. Compressing her lips, she forced her mouth into a parody of a sexy pout. She spent a few minutes practicing a variety of languid faces in the mirror, sucking in her cheeks and pursing her lips, while she efficiently brushed out her hair. She was wearing it straight tonight—long, heavy, so dark as to be almost black. Sweeping one side back behind her ear, she secured it with a rhinestone comb, emeralds and diamonds playing hide and seek with the light as she moved her head, the game echoed by matching earrings swinging from her lobes.

She had highlighted her creamy complexion with a whisper of blush and smudged a smokey-gray shadow at the corner of her green eyes, blending it upward to emphasize their almond shape and tilt, calling attention to her Polynesian ancestry.

And now for the coup de grace, Claire declared solemnly. Looking down, she carefully guided her feet into black high heels, taking a moment to balance herself on the skinny three-inch spikes. Pumps and low-heeled slings might be the fashion rage, but Claire had always declared that high heels were the one advantage to being only five-four. She loved the way they made her legs look—as if they went on forever—and she'd found that men had a certain weakness for them, too!

Claire was smiling rather wickedly to herself as the doorbell rang and she went to let David in, heels tapping out a knowing cadence on the hardwood floor.

Her eyes were sparkling with an inner excitement as she opened the door. David had been right—she was looking forward to this evening out. Her dress was perfect, the cool spring air was perfect, the choice of restaurant was perfect, and her companion? Was perfect, Claire had to admit as she swung open the door and saw David standing on her step, a long-stemmed rose in his hand.

The expensive cut of his suit fit his tall frame with the precision of custom tailoring, and its dark blue color was the perfect foil for his blond hair. David's quirky individualism was apparent in his choice of pink shirt and wildly patterned gray tie, and Claire could see a flash of turquoise suspenders as he held out the rose to her, the movement of his arm causing his unbuttoned jacket to swing open.

"Now I wish I'd gotten an orchid," he told her, his eyes openly admiring her. "This poor rose seems so ordinary compared to the way you look tonight."

"It's lovely," Claire replied, an unaccustomed feeling of shyness making her lower her gaze to the flower in her hand. She ran a caressing finger along one velvety petal, gently outlining its budding promise. David's rather simple compliment had disconcerted her.

David was a master when it came to complimenting women, his hyperbole knowing no bounds. But tonight his words had been lacking their usual extravagance. The look in his eyes and the tone of his voice conveyed explicitly how attractive he found her, without his having to resort to a string of adjectives. And, somehow, that very simplicity made Claire feel—special.

"I'll just go put this in some water and get my purse," she murmured.

"Wait." David held out a restraining hand. "I've got something to show you." He took her by the elbow and guided her outside onto the step next to him.

"What do you think?" he asked, pride swelling his voice.

Claire's intake of breath was audible as she followed his pointing finger. Parked in their driveway, right next to her ten-year-old family van, was a brand-new luxury sedan. Gray. Four doors. Gleaming dully with a new car shine, too expensive to do anything as gaudy as sparkle. It sat solidly on its tires among the weedy gravel of the driveway, overcoming its environment with an understated elegance, refinement and good breeding apparent even in the dusky halflight of approaching night.

Claire looked up at the man next to her, her eyes big, questioning.

"And paid for, Claire." David's voice was quiet. "In cash." His eyes locked with hers.

Claire knew immediately what he was referring to. The feeling of déjaà vu was instant and overwhelming and Claire was helplessly swept back to an evening exactly two years before.

Chapter Five

It had been the day after tax day and she was lying in her darkened bedroom, huddled in a miserable ball, a migraine splitting her skull and making unbearable flashes of light explode behind her clenched eyelids each time she moved her head. She was exhausted.

The day before had been its usual frantic chaos, a stream of belligerent clients waiting until the last possible minute to file their taxes, a token gesture of defiance against the herculean power of the IRS. And to make matters worse, Katy had been sick, running a fever and throwing up, forcing Claire to wash load after load of sheets and blankets, running back and forth between her office, Katy's bedroom and the laundry room in between clients.

She'd hoped that when David got home that evening he could give her a break, and she'd forced herself to keep going, watching the clock anxiously, praying the hands to five-thirty. But the minute he'd walked in the door from his construction job, he'd holed up in the study, hunched over his typewriter with the door shut, oblivious to everything but his story. He was on a roll—and sick kids, tax day, those things meant nothing to him. He couldn't be disturbed.

So now she lay in bed, thinking bitterly how unfair it was that his work always seemed to come before hers—especially when it was *her* work that paid the bills. How unfair it was that even Katy's illness couldn't penetrate his self-absorption when he was writing. Carefully she rolled over, trying not to move her head any more than necessary, giving fervent thanks to her mother who'd agreed to watch Katy for the day. Grandma was an angel when it came to recuperating kids and Claire couldn't imagine having to cope with Katy and a migraine at the same time.

And then there were the renters. Claire almost moaned aloud. She was supposed to be resting, relaxing, letting the pain melt away—but how could she relax when the tenants on the third floor had come that morning to announce they were moving out. That minute. Sorry about the stain on the carpet and what the cat did to the drapes—and the unpaid rent. How could she relax when her mind kept juggling their bills, trying to figure out how they were going to come up with enough extra that month to get the apartment cleaned and repaired and rented again. How they were going to get by without the income.

Her mind had started slogging through the options once again when she heard David come home, slamming the front door with a force that made her wince. Suddenly her bedroom was flooded with blinding light as he burst into the room and hit the switch, so excited he didn't even notice the way she paled sickeningly at the brightness and noise.

The magazine had bought his story! Wasn't it wonderful? Wasn't it fantastic? Couldn't she just jump up and down with joy? David dragged her out of bed, her weak protests not registering on him at all in the midst of his euphoria. He had something to show her. Outside. Come on. She'd be thrilled.

Claire stood reeling on the front step, clutching at David to keep upright, trying to get her eyes to focus on the source of so much jubilation. It was sitting in their driveway. It was fire engine red, a red blazing enough to make her squint. A sportscar, at least a dozen years old, with a dented rear fender and looking as though it had more than one hundred thousand miles on it.

David was dangling car keys in front of her face, trying to urge her down the steps. He couldn't wait to take her for a drive.

But Claire grabbed onto the railing and planted her feet, resisting with what was left of her meager strength. She tried to find her voice. "You—You bought this?"

"Isn't it great?" David was bouncing on his toes, grinning from ear to ear.

"How much?" Her voice was flat.

"Only fifteen-hundred dollars! Can you believe it? A steal!"

"Where did we get fifteen-hundred dollars?" The words were even deader this time.

Claire's marked lack of enthusiasm finally began to get through to him. A defensiveness stiffened his shoulders and stilted his speech. "The magazine said the check would be here in only three or four weeks..."

Claire waited.

"So I got a cash advance on our credit card."

It felt as if a hammer had hit her on the back of the head. She clenched her teeth against the pain and the surge of rage his words had produced. "You know that was our entire credit limit?" She needed all her willpower to keep her words coherent.

"Well, yeah, but—"

Claire didn't let him finish, cutting him off with sarcasm thick and bitter. "So, *Dr.* David, you're sure Katy doesn't have appendicitis, then?"

"What?" David's face was a mixture of confusion and alarm.

"Katy? Your daughter? The one who's been throwing up and running a fever and saying her stomach hurt. You decided, in your *infinite* wisdom, that it's just a stomach flu and that it's perfectly okay to take the credit card we save for emergencies and charge it to its limit, knowing damn well we don't have a *dime* of medical insurance?"

David's voice hardened. "I think you're overreacting, Claire. It's just for a few weeks until the check comes in."

"Oh, so now you're the *divine* David! Foreseeing the future—knowing that in the next 'few weeks' nobody's going to get sick or get in an accident." Claire's hand slashed through the air in the direction of the car. "Buying that—that *wreck* there was so important you'd put it before your family's welfare?"

"You know damn well we'd decided that if the story sold we'd buy a new car! We'd decided—"

"*We*, David?" Claire taunted. "I don't see any *we* here. I see *you* deciding to buy a car today. I see *you* deciding which car to buy. I see *you* deciding to borrow the money." Her voice broke as she felt a hysterical laugh rising in her throat, threatening to overpower the tears she was trying desperately to hold back. "I see you being so immature that you couldn't wait three damn weeks—three *lousy* weeks—needing instant gratification like a child. I see—"

Claire bit off her words, her anger so great she couldn't go on. Dark hair flying, she twirled and ran back into the house to their bedroom. Ignoring her throbbing head, she threw herself down onto her hands and knees next to the bed, feeling under it until her fingers closed on the handle of their battered suitcase. Blindly she began opening drawers, reaching for handfuls of his clothes, throwing them haphazardly into the suitcase.

David stood at their bedroom door, watching her silently, incredulously, as she clicked the brimming suitcase shut and heaved it off the bed. Dragging it across the floor, she shoved it unceremoniously against his knees, almost knocking him back under the force of her fury.

"You know what I see, David?" Each word was clipped, razor sharp, cutting ragged holes in the fabric of their marriage. "I see you getting the hell out of my life!"

So David had gone upstairs to the vacant third-floor apartment with the suitcase in one hand and a folding cot tucked under his arm. And somehow two years had passed.

The present pain of a thorn poking cruelly into her palm as she gripped the rose too tightly forced Claire to rapidly blink the two-year-old memory away. She was staring once again at the new gray car in front of her. A car he'd wanted her to know he'd paid for—in cash. Claire understood immediately that this was David's apology of sorts, for that night two years before—a kind of divorce anniversary present to her, an atonement for what he knew she perceived as his past sins.

Now he was waiting for a response from her; she could sense his tension.

"It's magnificent!" Claire made sure her voice conveyed her wholehearted approval of his choice and, immediately, she could feel the hand on her elbow relax. His apology had been accepted.

"But this?" she asked, tilting her head to give him a teasing look, trying to lighten the emotion-charged moment. "What about that black turbo thing you've talked about ever since I've known you?"

David shrugged his shoulders. "That's only a two seater—it wouldn't be very practical. Where would we put Katy?"

Claire tried to hide her surprise. Since when did David consider things such as practicality when it came to his wants? Since when did he even use words such as "practical"?

"But this beauty has plenty of room," he went on. "Lots of power, and a certain—authority, if I do say so myself. I thought it would fit my new image a little better than a twelve-year-old hot rod. Although I *am* going to miss you ferrying me all over town every time it broke down, you know." He grinned.

"Oh, and I'm certainly going to miss spending my weekends repairing it for you."

"What you're going to miss is feeling smug and self-righteous and I-told-you-so-ish. I think, secretly, you *loved* it when I couldn't get the damn thing to limp out of the driveway."

Claire laughed. "And I thought I'd hidden my feelings so well!"

David joined in her laughter. "Come on. Let's go wallow in luxury for an evening. We deserve it."

"Let me go put this in water, first." Claire gestured to the flower in her hand. She went into the kitchen and was busy filling a bud vase at the sink when the telephone rang.

"Hello?" Claire cradled the receiver between chin and shoulder while she dried her hands. "Oh, Lawrence, it's so good to hear from you." David was standing beside her and she shot him a look, turning so her back was to him, trying to maintain an illusion of privacy since he was very obviously going to listen to every word of her conversation.

"Yes, it was *very* considerate of you not to call this week. I really do appreciate you being so understanding. It's been a zoo around here." Claire glared at

David, holding her hand over the receiver so the little smooch-smooch sounds he was making with his pursed lips wouldn't carry over the line.

"Yes, I miss you, too." She twisted her head to try to avoid the tickling stream of air David was blowing into her free ear. "Oh, I would have loved to, but I'm going out tonight. With a friend."

She had to fight hard not to laugh at the exaggerated gagging motions David was making at her choice of the word *friend*. "In fact, I was just getting ready to head out the door. Yes. Call me tomorrow and we'll plan something. I've got to run. Uh-huh, that's nice. Bye. Stop that, you adolescent!" Claire pushed an elbow into David's side, trying to nudge him away and stop him from busily making a tiny braid in a section of her hair.

"Someone has to keep you from ruining your life," David told her complacently, admiring the silky shine of her hair as she raked her fingers through it to loosen his handiwork.

"I like my life just fine, thank you. Let's go." Claire picked up her evening bag from the counter and headed for the door, David following obediently at her heels.

"Marrying that boring old fuddy-duddy would have you in pearls and polyester before you knew what hit you," he persisted. "As your *friend,* I can't let you do it."

"I haven't said yes, yet." Dismayed, Claire bit her lip, immediately wishing she could take back the words. She'd just confirmed, in a roundabout way, that Lawrence had proposed, something she had no intention of discussing with David.

Once they were settled in the plush interior of the car, Claire firmly turned the topic away from her relationship with Lawrence and began admiring the car David was willing enough to let the conversation shift, trying to ignore the cold knot that had twisted in his stomach as Claire's chance words confirmed his fears.

For the second time that evening, David had surprised her. First, by his choice of car, and now by his behavior at dinner. They were circling the dance floor, Claire's feet following David's lead effortlessly, leaving her mind free to puzzle about the out-of-character attentiveness he'd shown her all night. It just wasn't like him at all!

He'd never so much as glanced at the cocktail waitress, Claire thought with fresh surprise. In her black miniskirt and high heels, making unsubtle efforts to catch his eye—Claire didn't believe he'd even noticed! The David she'd been married to wouldn't have been able to keep himself from harmlessly flirting with a waitress—any waitress. It was as natural to him as breathing. Of course, in the end, their service had suffered a little from his lack of response, but Claire found it a refreshing change, just the same.

And he'd been a superb conversationalist, flatteringly interested in her work, which was certainly a change from the old David. Over the years, he'd made it painfully clear that he found accounting a dull, uninspired occupation. Tonight he'd given her his full attention, making her feel fascinating and witty and—

desirable. Normally David's high-energy level would have his gaze wandering throughout the room, commenting acerbically on the other diners, telling anecdotes, doing his life-of-the-party number. Even for an audience of one.

A cynical part of her mind was telling her not to be too impressed with this novel behavior. David was like a chameleon, trying on and discarding roles to suit his purpose. Maybe tonight he was playing his how-to-win-back-a-wife role.

And doing a damn good job of it, Claire had to admit a few hours later when they finally arrived back home. She sent him upstairs to pick up Katy while she started a pot of coffee, still puzzling about the man, the almost stranger, she'd spent the evening with. Of course it had been two years since they'd spent an entire evening together this way—alone—without Katy to act as a buffer or a focusing point. Six hours to devote entirely to each other. That was probably more time than they'd spent alone together the whole last year of their marriage, Claire thought wryly. Was this the real David, the man he'd become over the past two years? Or was this just tonight's performance?

She watched him carry a sleep-limp Katy into her room and lay her down on the pink sheets. Carefully he untied her tennis shoes and slipped them off her feet, then pulled the pink comforter up to tuck under her chin. He dropped a kiss on her forehead and straightened up to smile at Claire standing in the doorway, reaching for the cup of coffee she held out for him, not embarrassed at all for her to witness the tender, loving way he'd cared for his child.

Claire shook her head. "I don't get this at all."

"Get what?" David followed her back to the living room where his long fingers immediately began tugging at his tie. Once it was loosened to his satisfaction he proceeded to slip off his dinner jacket, revealing the garish turquoise suspenders underneath, and seated himself comfortably on the couch.

"Get what?" he repeated, legs stretching out in front of him.

"Cars!" Claire said almost accusingly. "And waitresses. And since when do you care a fig about straight-line depreciation?"

"I've always liked depreciation, Claire, you know that." David's voice was deadpan. He didn't have the least idea what she was talking about.

Claire glared at him, his teasing not appreciated. She would have stamped her foot in frustration if she'd been the stamping type, and if she hadn't already kicked off her shoes. "I'm serious! Didn't you even notice that waitress tonight?"

"The waitress?" David repeated. A witty retort sprang automatically to his lips, something about "only having eyes for you," but he stopped himself. Claire was serious. This was not the time for flippant remarks.

"No," he replied instead. "I didn't really pay much attention."

"Why not?"

"I don't know, Claire!" This grilling was making him nervous. "What's this all about? Are you trying to tell me you're upset because I *didn't* flirt with a waitress?"

"Not upset, just confused." Claire worried a moment longer, narrowed eyes never leaving his face. "And when you went to buy a new car, you actually thought that turbo thing wouldn't be practical—I mean, you really used a word like 'practical'?"

David nodded gravely. Her intensity had rubbed off on him, prompting him to explain, "Naturally I did a little window-shopping, but I never really considered buying anything too extravagant."

"Why not?"

"Give me some credit, Claire," he said quietly. "Everyone has a fantasy they outgrow."

She digested this without comment, still standing in the middle of the room, small and dark and lovely—and concentrating on him fiercely. David bore her scrutiny unflinchingly, knowing he was being subjected to some kind of test, a test he wanted desperately to pass even though he didn't know the answers—or the questions.

"Is this you, David?" she said finally. "Or is this who you think I want you to be?"

"This is who *I* want to be, Claire."

But her disbelief was obvious. It showed on her face as clearly as if she'd shouted her doubts aloud.

Exasperated, David got up from the sofa and planted himself in front of her, looking down at her from his considerable height, as if his mere proximity could convince her. "I've spent the last couple of days thinking seriously about our talk the other night—when you gave me such a long list of all the things wrong with our marriage." A smile quirked the corner of his mouth. "If our being friends is more important to you than sex, more important to you than money, then it's time I gave some thought to how to be a friend. What it means—''

"A leopard can't change his spots so easily," Claire interrupted, sweeping away his explanation with a toss of her head.

"And you can't teach an old dog new tricks?" David suggested helpfully.

Claire's chin raised, squaring itself stubbornly. "Clichés don't get to be old for no reason," she insisted.

"But I'm not a leopard or a dog or a cliché—and I *can* change. Lord, Claire, I'm not like the IRS! It doesn't take an act of congress to get me to alter an opinion or an outlook or an attitude. People change every day of their lives! Do you really think *you're* the same person you were two years ago?"

"But my changes have been for myself—to make *me* happy. Trying to change yourself to make another person happy is never going to work. You've got to believe the change is right for *you* not for *me!*"

"It's right for both of us! Claire, Claire, you're making this so complicated. That analytical brain of yours is trying to dissect and study and evaluate—here, let me simplify it for you." He laid a hand on each of her shoulders and bent his head down slightly to better face her. "Having you for my wife is the most important thing in the world to me. I would change my religion if I thought it would help. I would change my politics, my hair color—anything! Well, anything but my sex," he couldn't resist adding with a grin.

"Hah! I knew you couldn't be serious for a minute!" Claire swatted him on the arm and tried to pull away, unable to keep an answering smile from curving her own lips.

This was getting too serious, anyway, she thought. She didn't need to be having these kinds of conversations with him. This supposed change to a mature, responsible, practical—well, maybe that was going too far, but he *was* behaving semiadult lately, she conceded—it was all just window-dressing with no underlying commitment. His true colors showed the minute he let his guard down.

And if she needed further proof that the same old David was lurking not far beneath the surface, the way his hands had begun to slide caressingly down her arms provided it. True to form, he couldn't let a single opportunity go by without trying to seduce her back into his life, without trying to breathe the ever-present spark between them into a blaze. He took a personal delight in reducing that "analytical brain" of hers to a mass of sensation-overloaded receptors, incapable of thought, let alone reason.

Claire waited for the inevitable. Perversely she found herself anticipating the moment when his lips would meet hers, when she could press herself to him and savor the hard, male lines of his body. David raised a hand, and with excruciating tenderness, he lifted a strand of hair off her cheek and tucked it behind her ear. She waited for his hand to continue to her nape, to tangle in her hair, to steady her head for his kiss. She found herself swaying forward, her eyes closing automatically.

The light brush of his lips on her forehead had her immediately opening them again, wide with astonishment. And when he stepped back, dropping his hands from her, she had to consciously keep her mouth from opening, too.

"It's getting late. I'd better be going," David said. "Happy Anniversary." He retrieved his suit coat and headed for the door, leaving her standing in the middle of her living room, literally flat-footed, her nylon-clad feet rooted to the carpet in surprise.

Claire stared after his departing back, curiously deflated and seriously confused.

Winter was back with a vengeance the next morning, seeming all the colder for the few days of mock-spring weather at the start of the week. Claire gave the bottom of the trash can a couple of quick thumps, watching the spirals of adding machine tape uncurl into the garbage can, then hurried back up the driveway and started up the steps. Naomi chose that moment to leave her own apartment, obviously dressed for jogging in her sweatsuit.

"How can you even *think* about jogging in this cold!" Claire called up in greeting. "You're going to freeze!"

"I'll warm up soon enough, never fear," the older woman assured her. She paused a moment on the landing outside Claire's door to pull on a pair of gloves. "So how was the big night out?" she asked, busily working her fingers into their neon fuzz.

"It was really nice. Thanks so much for watching Katy."

"No problem. The kids all got along great. Where'd you go?"

"The Garden," Claire pushed open her door and beckoned Naomi inside. She was beginning to shiver in only jeans and T-shirt.

"Wow! Even a newcomer like me has heard of The Garden. Is it as expensive as they say?"

"Worse."

"Were you guys celebrating or something?" Naomi asked as she followed Claire toward the kitchen, declining an offer of coffee with a shake of her head.

"Sort of." Claire poured a cup for herself. "Yesterday was the two-year anniversary of our separation."

Naomi's eyebrow lifted. "Strange thing to celebrate, if you don't mind my saying."

"We have a strange relationship—as I'm sure you've noticed." Claire sighed. "I hope you realize how lucky you are. Married to the Captain, I mean. He seems so...so dependable."

"Like a rock," Naomi agreed. "Of course, you need a man like that when you marry the military. It's not exactly the life for the security conscious."

"Hmm, I suppose not. I thought being married to a struggling writer was bad, but military life—all those moves! I'd be a neurotic mess wondering when and where we'd be sent next."

"Oh, the moves weren't so bad. Now the wars— they were a different story." Naomi's face took on a pinched look. "Korea was bad. Vietnam was worse."

Claire felt a shiver of horror run down her spine at the stark understatement. My God, if that wasn't the ultimate lack of security! she thought. Never knowing when a war would take your husband away—perhaps permanently! Suddenly she felt ashamed, in front of this woman, about the fuss she'd made over a tame-by-comparison trip to Alaska. Maybe David and his bear weren't so serious after all.

"How could you stand that?" she asked. It was not a rhetorical question. Claire couldn't imagine such a life.

But Naomi just shrugged, the tight lines around her mouth relaxing. "What we won't do for love, huh?"

"Love!" Claire scoffed. "Love's not enough. Not near enough! To put up with the uncertainty, the fear, the worry— No way!"

Naomi blinked. It seemed she'd hit a sore spot. Claire was positively glowering at her. "I've always found love to be a pretty motivating thing," she said mildly. " 'Love conquers all'—and all that."

"Now you sound just like David." Claire didn't want to have clichés quoted to her, regardless of her own reliance on them the night before.

"We romantics have to stick together." Naomi decided she'd better change the subject before Claire's dark look blackened further. "Well, I guess I better get moving before I decide it's too cold for a run, after all." She made a few inane remarks about the weather, took a moment to settle her earphones in place, then with a wave of a still-gloved hand headed for the door.

Claire left her coffee untouched on the counter. She picked up the empty trash can and carried it back to her office. Time to get to work. She still had to process the midmonth payroll for Lawrence's office supply stores.

Love conquers all! Hah! she thought as she flipped the switch to her computer and pulled out Lawrence's file. She'd had just about enough of temperamental writers and death-defying soldiers. Office supplies—now there was something safe and solid and totally dependable.

Chapter Six

Being totally dependable, Lawrence called that afternoon at 3:00—as he had every Friday afternoon since they'd started dating—to arrange plans for the evening. "Wear something nice," he'd told her. "We're going somewhere special."

And since by now Claire knew what Lawrence's definition of "nice" was, she met him at the door dressed in a chic black dress, her hair in a smooth roll at her nape, small gold studs in her ears—the picture of understated elegance. As always, when going out with Lawrence, she'd done her eye makeup carefully, downplaying any suggestion of the exotic. Although he had never said anything, Claire knew that, unlike David, Lawrence was not attracted to the hula-dancer image.

No, Lawrence was nothing if not conservative, Claire thought, lifting her cheek for his kiss of greeting. Of average height and slightly stocky build, his gray suit and careful navy tie, black Italian shoes with their expensive luster, touch of white at the temples of his fresh-from-the-barber brown hair—they all proclaimed unabashedly that here was a successful businessman, a capitalist, a conservative. And Claire had always found it an attractive combination.

Lawrence might not have flair, but he had common sense; he might lack a certain boyish charm, but he was loyal to a fault. Charismatic…maybe not, but he was hardworking and kind—and why am I defending him? Claire asked herself, stopping her mental cataloging in disgust. And against whom? She didn't have to explain herself to anyone! She liked Lawrence enormously and if she was seriously considering his marriage proposal, it was nobody's business but her own—and Katy's.

"I *said* I have two surprises for you," Lawrence said, his tone making it clear he was repeating himself.

Claire started. "Surprises?"

"Here's one," Lawrence said. For the first time she noticed that he was holding out a small, gift-wrapped package.

With a sound of pleasure, Claire took the long rectangular box and eased off the expensive silver paper. Lawrence watched with a pleased look on his face as she opened the jeweler's case to reveal a strand of exquisite pearls, creamy white against the dark blue velvet interior. He waited, his look becoming even more self-congratulatory, as Claire lifted the necklace out, obviously speechless with delight.

Speechless Claire definitely was, but not for the reason Lawrence thought. *He'd have you in pearls and polyester before you knew what hit you.* That's what David had said last night. Pearls and polyester. She tried to push the thought away. How ungrateful could you get? Besides, she loved pearls, she thought defiantly.

"I love it!" Claire declared firmly. "It's the most beautiful thing I've ever seen." Obediently she turned around to let Lawrence fasten the clasp behind her neck. But as Lawrence encircled her throat she found herself swallowing hard, convulsively, fighting a sudden feeling of suffocation that swept over her as the weight of the pearls dragged expensively against her skin. Don't be silly, she chided, but she couldn't stop her fingers from lifting to fiddle with the smooth beads, tugging at them the way a man loosens a too-tight tie at the end of a long workday.

"Perfect," Lawrence proclaimed. He took a step back and surveyed her with appreciation. "You'll be the most beautiful woman there."

"Where's there?" Claire managed to clear her throat enough to ask.

"That's the second surprise." The self-satisfied look was back. "Tonight we'll be dining at the best restaurant in Minneapolis."

"Not—"

"That's right! The Garden!" Lawrence beamed. "Surprised? You were just saying last month how you wanted to try it. So I thought tonight would be the perfect time—now that all your tax work is over with. Sort of a celebration, hmm?"

Claire forced a smile. Another night of celebration at The Garden. How nice.

"Just another half hour!" Claire tried not to snap. "Please, Katy! Thirty more minutes and I'll be finished—then I'll help you with your puzzle. I promise. Not another word!" she threatened as Katy opened her mouth for one more try at getting her mother's attention.

Convinced Claire meant business this time, Katy moped back to her room. Claire watched her leave the office with equal amounts of annoyance and guilt. It hadn't been a very fun Saturday for the child, but Claire had really needed to spend the morning catching up on her work. She'd let some of her regular clients' accounts slide while she'd concentrated on tax returns. If only Katy would realize the more times she interrupted, the longer it was going to take!

And it would go a lot faster, Claire fretted, if she could keep her mind on her work and get this damned ledger to balance! Taking a deep breath, she scanned the column of figures once again, looking for her error. But she was tired and was grouchy and she couldn't concentrate—because she kept thinking about last night. Or, more specifically, she kept comparing last night with the night before that. Comparing her evening with Lawrence to her evening with David. And trying not to admit that she had been a little, well . . . bored last night.

Bored? The numbers in front of her blurred as, once again, she allowed her mind to drift back over the two evenings—same restaurant, but different men—and totally different atmospheres. Had she really been bored with Lawrence? Or was it just that two nights out in a row had taken their toll? But when Lawrence had kissed her good-night last night, quite thoroughly, too, she hadn't been nearly as affected as when David had simply brushed his lips against her forehead. She hadn't wanted—

Now, wait just a minute! Claire scolded herself. She'd never for a moment denied the overwhelming physical attraction she still felt for David, nor tried to pretend that she felt any strong physical desire for Lawrence. So it wasn't fair to base the—the "wrongness" of last night on a purely physical response. It was something more than that. It was the way she couldn't wait to remove the pearl necklace as soon as she got home. It was the way Lawrence's hair was exactly a half-inch above his collar—she'd never seen it more and she'd never seen it less. It wasn't natural! It was irritating. She couldn't imagine why she'd never noticed it before.

Ah! There it was. She'd transposed 34 to 43. No wonder it wouldn't balance. Thank God her subconscious was paying attention to her work. Quickly she typed the correction and with a few more keystrokes started the computer processing the general ledger entries. Almost through now—spend some time puzzling with Katy then maybe they'd both lay down for a nap. Katy had stayed last evening with Grandma and Grandpa and there was no doubt she'd been able to get them to postpone bedtime for hours—she could probably use a nap, too.

Lawrence had said he'd call later in the day to see if she felt like renting a video and spending a quiet evening at home with Katy. But right now that idea seemed about as exciting as—well, as last night had been. Damn David, anyway! Claire swore forlornly, storing her program and flipping off the computer. She'd almost grown used to the idea that she'd never find another man sexually attractive, but it plain old wasn't fair if David's very *personality* made it impossible for her to even find pleasure in another man's *company!*

She'd been seeing too much of David, lately. That was the problem, Claire reminded herself, knowing she'd come to that very same conclusion only last week. She'd enjoyed dating Lawrence well enough these past few months. Well, enough to consider marrying the man! It was only because she and David had been together too often that she was having so much trouble now. She'd simply overdosed on charisma, that was all. She needed to remember that a steady diet of David's charm had gotten just as boring, just as irritating, after a while, as Lawrence's well-trimmed hair seemed now.

So. Once again. No more David. No more meals with David—not breakfast, lunch or supper. Period. Strictly landlord/tenant from now on. Just the occasional plugged toilet. They were divorced. She was practically engaged. No more kisses, on the forehead or otherwise.

Satisfied that she was on the right track back to normalcy, Claire left the office and made her way toward Katy's room, wondering if the child would protest too much about soup for lunch again. Turning in midstride, Claire made a quick detour to the kitchen to see if some new, more appetizing flavor might have somehow appeared on the shelf. She was staring at the same old array of cans in the pantry when the doorbell rang.

She didn't bother rushing to answer it. Sure enough, she had barely started in the direction of the door when Katy, as usual, came bursting headlong down the hallway. "I'll get it!" she yelled, careening around Claire and throwing open the door. "Hi! Want to come help me with my puzzle?" she demanded.

By now Claire, too, had reached the door to see Naomi Maxwell and her husband on her front step. "No, they don't want to help you with your puzzle," Claire told her daughter, physically moving her aside so their guests could enter.

"Well, not right now anyway. But," Naomi held up a hand, forestalling Katy's protests, "we have something even better in mind."

"What?" Katy asked excitedly. "What?"

"Have you already had lunch?"

"Nope. Mom hasn't opened up any soup yet."

"Perfect. Because there's a new store opening today at the mall—a Mexican food chocolate chip cookie place."

"You're kidding." Claire's nose wrinkled as she tried to imagine the combination.

"Bizarre, huh?" Naomi laughed. "It's called Choco-Taco. Today's their grand opening. We thought it sounded better than a tuna fish sandwich so we're on our way. Why don't you guys come with us?"

"Oh, we'd love to, but I should probably get another hour or so worth of work done later on this afternoon. I'm pretty behind."

"They're giving away free samples," Naomi said, temptingly.

But Claire still shook her head and smiled.

"Oh, come on, Claire! You work too hard. You're turning yourself into an old lady—and poor Katy, too!" Naomi's voice held just a touch of asperity.

"No, really, I can't—" Involuntarily her glance followed Naomi's down to rest on Katy's face. And it wasn't just the face of a disappointed child Claire saw staring back up at her: It was the face of a child *expecting* to be disappointed. Katy had known Claire was going to refuse before she'd even opened her mouth!

Claire frowned. Was she really such an old stick-in-the-mud? Was she so predictable in denying these spontaneous outings that a five-year-old could second-guess her? Good grief, even the Captain looked ready for an afternoon's play dressed in a gaudy Hawaiian-print shirt and khaki pants—although the pleats in both were knife sharp.

"Chocolate tacos did you say?" she asked weakly.

"Chocolate *and* tacos, Mom," Katy said in exasperation.

Claire groaned. "I know my stomach is never going to forgive me for this."

"Really?" Katy's face lit up. At her mother's nod, the little girl positively ran to get on her shoes and coat and in no time at all they were heading out the door, ready to join the Maxwell's for a lunch trip to the mall.

"Do you want to take two cars?" Claire asked as they reached the driveway. But the Maxwells had already walked past their car—and now they were walking past her beat-up old clunker. "No, Katy, that's Daddy's car," Claire called out as the child started pulling on the door handle of the new gray sedan. But then the latch was opened from the inside and the door pushed wide, David reaching across from where he was sitting in the driver's seat to hold the door for his daughter.

Naomi and the Captain settled themselves comfortably in the roomy back seat and everyone waited for Claire, who was standing stock-still in the gravel, to slide in next to Katy.

"Come on, Momma," Katy called, scrambling over to stick her head out the open door. "I'm starving!"

Claire tried to glare at Naomi through the rolled-up glass of the back door but the older woman refused to catch her eyes, serenely turning to say something to her husband. Well, it was too late to back out now, Claire thought with resignation. As Naomi had known it would be! She plumped down and pulled the door shut with unnecessary vigor. So much for her minutes-old resignation to spend no more time with David. This was the second time in a matter of a week or so that she'd vowed to put more distance between them—only to end up practically in his lap!

"Put on your seat belt," she told Katy, reaching to help her with the buckle. Her head was turned just enough to see the little conspiratorial smile David shared with Naomi in the rearview mirror before he started the engine. So! Naomi had gone over to the enemy camp! Well, Claire was on to them now and she wouldn't be so easily maneuvered again.

But at the mall, munching on free samples of tacos and cookies, she found it impossible to keep herself from being marshaled into place as they wandered from shop to shop. Naomi and the Captain walked ahead, keeping Katy firmly between them, which forced Claire to walk side by side with David.

"No fair!" she snarled at him through clenched teeth as, once again, Naomi managed to adroitly, though nonchalantly, position her trio so that it would be awkward for Claire to move up and join them. "It's two against one!"

"All's fair in love and war." David grinned back, unperturbed, offering her his last chocolate chip cookie.

"Then this is war, and I don't take food from the enemy."

"Claire, the way you cook, you should take food from anybody that offers."

Claire couldn't help laughing, shaking her head at the impossibility of staying mad at David for long. What the hell, she decided. She was already here, she'd gotten a free, if unorthodox, lunch and Katy was having a ball—why not just relax and enjoy a pleasant Saturday afternoon. It was sort of fun to window-shop, dragging Katy out of one toy store after another and the Captain out of every bookstore they passed.

"Momma, Momma, look it!" Katy cried suddenly, running up to a window that had row after row of color televisions displayed, all tuned to the same channel so that a coyote was falling off a sandstone cliff simultaneously on every set. *Beep! Beep!* a dozen roadrunners honked, churning into a dozen clouds of dust. "Look it! Color! Color TVs! How come these pictures don't have little white dot-things all over them like our TV does?"

David sputtered with laughter. "Yeah! How come, Momma?" he teased. "Could it be that these TVs aren't a hundred years old?" He bent down so his face was next to his daughter's. "Katy, will you please tell your mother it's time to buy a new television? Tell her that *none* of your friends have even *heard* of black-and-white TVs."

"We can't *possibly* afford a new TV!" Claire started to say with a shake of her head.

But the words were already being said! In a high child's voice—but with exactly the same tone, the same emphasis, the same phrasing that Claire was going to use.

"We can't *possibly* afford a new TV!" Katy was telling her father, her young face serious.

Claire froze, staring down at a child's face echoing an adult's worry, and she felt something inside her snap.

"Yes! We can! Katy, we *can* afford a new television." Claire felt as shocked to hear herself say the words as the faces that turned to stare at her looked.

What was she saying! "I mean...I've been thinking it was about time to get one just the other day," Claire said, lying. "Why don't we...umm, why don't we look around here a little bit and see what they have and maybe..." She swallowed hard. "Maybe we can buy one next week."

"A new TV?" Katy asked incredulously, wide eyes never leaving her mother's face. "With color in it?"

Claire nodded, feeling the heat of embarrassment begin to flame in her cheeks as even Naomi and the Captain turned to stare at her.

"Really?" four voices asked in unison.

"What?" she cried. "What's so hard to believe? We need a new television. So what?"

The three adults had the grace to look flustered.

"Oh, now, Claire," David began in a placating tone. "It's just that you've had that old thing for so long and, well, you're not exactly known for...what I mean is, is you're pretty...frugal. About money, I mean—"

"Daddy says you're tighter than bark on a tree," Katy supplied helpfully.

Claire felt the heat on her face raise another degree. Naomi and her husband became very busy, all of a sudden, looking at a display of video recorders and David was doing his level best not to laugh aloud—she could see the way his shoulders were beginning to shake from the effort to hold it in.

"Is that what Daddy says?" Claire inquired, fighting to keep her tone mild. "Well, why don't we go find a salesman to tell us about these televisions?" she suggested evenly.

They entered the store, tensions outwardly eased, eagerly comparing notes about screen size and brand names. But Claire only listened with half an ear to the salesman's earnest pitch, her mind still trying to adjust to the fact that she'd just agreed, in front of witnesses, to spend several hundred dollars. Why had she said yes? And why was it so hard?

Claire was introspective and quiet for the remainder of the afternoon, rehashing the scene in front of the television store over and over in her mind. Katy had known she would say no to Naomi's lunch invitation, and she'd not only known Claire would say no to a new television, but she'd also known exactly how, word-for-word, Claire would say it! Was this really how Katy saw her? And how the rest of them saw her—even Naomi and the Captain, who had only known her a few weeks? A workaholic miser? A penny-pincher to the point of being cheap?

They *could* afford a new television. And God knows they certainly needed one! Then why had the first words out of her mouth been that they couldn't? Or at least they would have been the first words if Katy hadn't beat her to it. Being frugal during tight times was admirable, it was how she was raised, careful and cautious with money—and Lord knows she'd had some tight times with David—but times weren't so tight now. So how come the first thing she thought of was "I can't afford it"? Self-denial for the sake of self-denial served no purpose.

Claire had been embarrassed to see herself reflected in those four faces that had stared at her so incredulously at the idea of her buying a new television.

And her feelings had been hurt. But most of all, she
didn't like knowing that, perhaps, they were right. Just
look at the wonderful time Katy was having today, she
thought as they all strapped on rented ice skates and
skidded around the mall's indoor rink. When was the
last time she'd done something like this with Katy? But
she was always so busy with work: the phone, everyone wanting it done yesterday! a part of her protested, trying to make excuses. Were all those
"they's," really more important than the way Katy
was right now? Claire demanded of herself. Katy, pink
cheeked and giggling, supported the Captain while his
ankles wobbled dangerously, spinning herself dizzy in
the middle of the rink.

What had happened to her? "A penny saved is a
penny earned." "Watch the pennies and the dollars
will take care of themselves." Had she taken all those
clichés she'd been raised to value, the Protestant work
ethic she'd been taught to be proud of, and perverted
them to the point where her own daughter was being
deprived?

Claire's musing lasted until they returned home and
each went to their respective floors, calling goodbyes
and thank-yous and I-had-a-great-time. Well, one
thing was for certain, she thought, still mulling it over
as she hung up their coats in the hall closet—they were
going to buy a new television. Katy had disappeared
into the living room and had the old set on now. Claire
glanced quickly at the clock to see what programs
would be on. Oh, no, she thought guiltily, they'd returned home too late to get Lawrence's phone call!
Damn! Oh, well, par for the day. But then another

thought struck her and Claire found herself actually smiling a ghost of a smile—they'd eaten so many choco-tacos, she wasn't going to have to cook supper tonight!

"Checkmate," David cried triumphantly, moving his little silver cavalryman forward a square.

The Captain shook his white head. "It's not checkmate when you only captured an infantryman like that. Besides, you're supposed to say 'surrender.' Checkmate's for chess."

"Oh." David consulted the yellow legal pad on the table beside him where he'd scribbled notes concerning the finer points of the Captain's war game. "How about if I take a battalion around your... your whatchamacallit—your rear end there."

"My flank. And you can only do that if you roll a pair of sixes."

"Oh." David stared at his few remaining pewter pieces, sadly outnumbered by the Captain's superior forces lined up in front of them. He fingered the dice, considering his options. "Can I surrender right now?" he finally asked.

"You might as well seeing as how you've hardly been fit to call an enemy today!" Sam Maxwell snorted. He leaned back in his chair and fixed the younger man with a stare that had quailed many a private over the years. "Your mind's obviously not on the game. What's the matter?" The question was barked out.

David found himself fighting the urge to sit up straighter. He knew that the Captain's gruff manner was more habit than anything else. The man didn't really mean to make people snap to attention whenever he spoke. He couldn't help the way years of conditioning had made his every statement sound as if it was an order.

"Nothing's really the matter," David hedged. "I'm just a little preoccupied, that's all."

"Preoccupied? If you hadn't lucked out and received air support when you did I would have annihilated your ground forces in the shortest battle in history." His eyes narrowed. "You and Naomi aren't hatching up some new way to shanghai your missus again are you?"

David laughed. "Not yet, but I wouldn't be surprised if your wife's not plotting something as we speak. She's quite an ally."

"Good woman to have in your corner when it comes to romancing and such," Sam agreed. "So, out with it. What else is making you such a lousy field commander today?"

David's shoulders slumped and he rested his elbows on the table. "I'm having a bout of writer's block, I guess." He sighed. "I heard from my editor yesterday and he wants some revisions on the last few chapters I sent him—but, I don't know, I just can't see the story going his way at all!" He shook his head and a crease marred his forehead.

"Did you tell this editor fellow that?"

David made a wry sound. "Oh, I told him, all right. But, well, editors have ideas of their own—and since they're the ones who decide whether or not to buy your book..."

He let the sentence hang and the Captain nodded, understanding his predicament.

"You know, it's strange," David continued, almost to himself. "I sweated bullets with *The Green of Spring*—agonized over every word. But this second story has moved right along from the start, been almost easy—I was really pleased with it. And now my editor pretty much says it's trash—these last couple chapters, anyway." David's voice sounded pained. "He wants a complete rewrite. Two months worth of work down the drain!"

"Then I wouldn't be sitting here messing around with toys and old retired men, if I were you," the Captain said matter-of-factly. "I'd be pounding my fingers on some typewriter keys."

David blinked in surprise. He'd expected just a little sympathy. After all, writer's block was a serious and well-documented malady.

"I'm waiting for some inspiration, I guess." He shrugged, trying to dismiss the subject lightly.

But the Captain would have none of it. "Inspiration, my foot!" He began to gather up the intricately designed toy soldiers, laying them carefully in a little padded box. "We had a saying in the force—about life being one part inspiration and ninety-nine parts perspiration."

David's smile was vaguely condescending. "Well, that's the service, this is—this is art!"

"Art, shmart. It's your job. You have a responsibility to your craft, if nothing else. You can't just float along waiting for inspiration to come hit you over the head." He waved a mounted soldier at him for emphasis. "What're your goals, boy? Your purpose? Where are you going with this writing business?"

David opened his mouth to stammer something, *anything* in response to the Captain's barrage. But his mind was blank! For one of the few times in his life, David didn't have an easy answer, a flip, light, one-liner. The Captain, just as his editor had been on the phone earlier, wasn't the least bit influenced by his charm or his wit or the good-ol'-boy routine that had served him so well in the past.

What were his goals? David found he didn't have any answer for that at all. Always before he'd been able to supply the pat phrase, "I want to be a famous writer." Well, now he was—what next?

David just sat there, staring helplessly at the older man, suddenly feeling as in control of his life as the toy soldiers the Captain was picking up and filing away, closing the lid on the case, leaving them in the dark.

Chapter Seven

It was all well and good to say you'd spend no more time with a man, but when you shared a house and a child with that man it was easier said than done. Of course, she could have paid to have the television delivered, Claire admitted as she watched David manhandle the heavy cardboard box into the living room. But David *had* offered to go pick it up, and she did hate having to pay that extra twenty-five dollars.

"Thank you so much for doing this for us, David."

"Sure," he grunted, letting the carton sink heavily down to the floor. "Whew! You must have gone all out and got the wide-screen model or something, huh?"

"It's a pretty nice set." Claire smiled smugly. She and Katy had had a wonderful time last night picking out the new color television. An *expensive* one, too, she wanted to tell him. With remote control. A name brand—none of this generic stuff. Hah! Make her feel cheap will they! She'd show them!

And David was suitably impressed when he finally managed to pry the box open and wrestle the set from its cocoon of foam packing. "Nice!" He whistled. He shifted the old black-and-white television from its stand and shoved it unceremoniously into a corner of the room, then he carefully centered the new set in its place.

It certainly did look good, Claire had to admit, admiring its wood cabinet and sleek, space-age-looking control panel.

"Did you notice it has one of those automatic color things," she asked proudly.

But David didn't hear her. He had searched through the foam until he found the instruction booklet and was now leafing through the pages of schematic diagrams with a comic look of dismay on his face. Tentatively he went to peer behind the set, fumbling for one of the wires leading to the antennae.

"Here, give that to me," Claire said with a laugh, taking the wire he was examining as if it were some exotic snake.

"Gladly!" He handed Claire the instruction booklet, too. "It's all yours. Why don't I go fix us a bite to eat while you wire up the evening's entertainment?"

She shook her head. "I already have some stew heating on the stove."

"I'll go give it a stir then," David said affably. "See if I can doctor up that canned stuff so it's edible."

"And just what makes you think it's canned?" Claire demanded. "I *can* cook a few things, you know. Stew isn't exactly soufflé!"

But David paid her no mind and continued on his way to the kitchen, forcing Claire to scramble to her feet. "I need a screwdriver from the junk drawer," she told him, darting past to enter the kitchen first. She planted herself in front of the counter by the stove, rummaging through the top drawer—trying to hide the two empty cans sitting on the countertop.

"Claire, Claire." David sighed. He lifted her up bodily and moved her aside. "'Beef stew, chunky style,'" he read aloud from the can he had gingerly picked up, using only two fingers.

Claire didn't appreciate his attitude a bit. She didn't continually make him feel inferior because he couldn't so much as hammer a nail straight, did she? "You're welcome to stay for supper," she told him stiffly.

"But Claire!" A mock look of horror came over his face at her offer. "I thought we'd been getting along so well lately! I thought we were friends! Why would you want to inflict *beef stew, chunky style* on me!"

That did it! Claire slammed the drawer shut with a swing of her hip and turned to face him, pointing the screwdriver threateningly. "I'll have you know, David Olson, that I am *not* that bad of a cook!"

"Since when!"

"Naomi has been giving me a few pointers. I even made a pot roast the other night and it wasn't the least bit dried out. So there!" She knew she sounded childish, but she'd had enough of this being put down for her spending habits, her working habits, her cooking.

"In fact," she added, her injured feelings making her bold. "I'll even go so far as to invite you to supper tomorrow."

David didn't even bother to try to look enthusiastic at the prospect.

"I'll fix something special. Something that will amaze you!"

"Like what?"

"It's a surprise," she told him, her chin lifting itself to a haughty angle, daring him to laugh! He didn't have to sound so damned skeptical!

Naturally, since she could read a cookbook, Claire could cook—after a fashion. But to say her meals were uninspired would be putting it mildly. She'd never really enjoyed cooking and thought it was a waste of time—all those hours of preparation for something that was bolted down in a matter of minutes. So she'd never bothered to learn more than a few basic recipes—enough to keep her and Katy from starving and that was about it. She sent up a quick prayer that Naomi would be able to come up with some recipe she could handle.

"Okay. I'll give it a try. I'm always ready to take a dare." He grinned at her. "Now, why don't you and your screwdriver go back to your new TV and I'll work some culinary magic on this chunky stuff and we'll eat. Okay?"

"Okay," she agreed, somewhat mollified. Returning to the living room, she squeezed behind the set and began connecting wires.

Later, after a meal of surprisingly good stew, they sprawled on the couch munching on microwave popcorn—something even Claire could fix well—watching one program after another. Katy was entranced at first but it wasn't long before she fell asleep on the floor, and Claire had to admit she was getting a little bored herself when yet another silly sitcom about a single parent with children just too precious, too precocious to be believable came on. She glanced over at David who seemed to be staring intently at the program, but she knew him well enough to know he wasn't paying the least bit of attention.

"Do you want me to turn it off?"

"Hmm?"

"The show. I don't think you're really watching it, either. Do you want me to turn it off?"

"Oh, I don't know. It seems a shame to turn off such a beautiful picture, even if it is a stupid program. Why don't you just turn the volume all the way down and we can admire the lovely colors?"

Claire laughed and got up to get the remote from Katy and turned off the set. Settling back down next to him, she once again sensed his preoccupation. "You're awfully quiet. Something bothering you? Besides dreading to eat my cooking tomorrow, I mean."

But her attempt at lightness failed. David's somber look deepened. "Mainly I've just been sitting here wondering how trash like that gets on the air." He waved a hand toward the television. "And I've been thinking about some new ideas my editor wants me to use in the book, trying to figure out how to keep my story from ending up as canned and stale as that show was." He explained to her about his editor's criticisms. "I mentioned it to the Captain, and he pretty much raked me over the coals—told me to stop whining and get on with it."

"Really!" Claire couldn't imagine the Captain saying that many words at one time.

David nodded. "He asked all kinds of uncomfortable questions, making it sound like I spend all my time sitting around twiddling my thumbs, like— Claire?" David broke off suddenly, interrupting himself. "What did you want to be when you grew up?"

"A ballerina," she answered promptly.

"No, I'm serious."

"So am I. I've always wanted to be a ballerina." She couldn't help smiling at his incredulous look. "Oh, I *know* I'm a dull, boring accountant, and too old and too short, but there's a part of me that will always be waiting in the wings for that first audition with some ballet troupe— And what has this got to do with anything?"

David didn't answer, and his look became even more brooding. He hadn't known that about Claire— about his own wife! How could he not have known that? What had they talked about for all those years of their marriage?

Him.

His goals, his plans, his wants—him, him, him! David was startled by the sudden revelation. He felt his face grow warm and his insides squirm uncomfortably at this unexpected look at himself. Had he really been that self-absorbed?

"David? What is it?" Claire asked worriedly. She'd never seen him so serious.

"Do you think I'm immature? Lacking direction? Unmotivated?"

"What?"

"A goof-off! A—a—" His lips twisted bitterly. "Will you look at that—I'm out of adjectives. And I call myself a writer!"

"Of course I don't think that! I think you're talented, and caring and—and—" Claire found herself stuttering to a close, unable to continue, knowing that, indeed, she had labeled David all those things at one time or another.

David heard her answer in her silence. "I thought so." He got briskly to his feet, knocking over the bowl of popcorn balanced on the couch between them. "Well, I better get busy!" His voice was falsely bright. "It seems I have some revisions to write!" He gave her a quick peck on the cheek and was gone.

Slowly Claire began to pick up the fluffy white kernels from the carpet. David was becoming more and more confusing to her. She'd never known him to be introspective before. This complex, complicated man she was seeing bore no resemblance to the husband she'd known, had always thought she knew as well as she knew herself. She sighed, settling on the floor next to her sleeping daughter, balancing the bowl of popcorn on her lap, she reached for the remote control and pushed the Power button.

When the phone rang that Friday afternoon Claire automatically glanced up at the clock. Three o'clock. Right on schedule, she thought with a prick of irritation, reaching for the receiver to talk to Lawrence.

"It looks like I'm going to have to take a rain check on tonight," she told him. "Tonight's Katy's school play. She's so excited. There's no way I can miss it."

"What time does it start? I'll give you a lift."

"Oh. Well, no, that's okay." Claire found herself hedging at the unexpected offer. "Uh, we already have a ride."

Silence greeted this information. Lawrence was waiting for an explanation.

"Yes, David's going to take us!" Claire admitted reluctantly, hearing his disapproval loudly in the continuing silence. Damn it all! Why did Lawrence always make her feel guilty every time she mentioned David's name? He was Katy's father, after all! Naturally he'd want to see his daughter in her first school play!

"It's just that Katy's a tree, you see." She hurried on. "There're leaves everywhere and it's really messy and...and everything." Lawrence and Katy got along well enough, but he wasn't exactly child-oriented, and childish messes such as gluey, construction-paper leaves falling all over the expensive leather seats of his car tended to make him nervous.

"I think I could stand a few leaves." Lawrence's tone reproved her.

"Of course, but, well, I've already promised Katy we'd go with David and—"

"But it's Friday night!" Lawrence protested. "You know we always spend Friday night together!"

"I know, I know." She tried to soothe him, once again feeling strangely irritated. She had always admired Lawrence's organized, scheduled, efficient approach to life, but tonight she found his lack of flexibility annoying. "It's just that this Friday something else has come up, that's all. We'll have to make it another night."

"I see." Again there was silence on the line, which, this time, Claire didn't rush to fill. "Then I guess I'll see you when you come in to the office with the accounts," Lawrence said, finally conceding defeat. "We can plan something more definite then."

"That would be great." Relieved Claire hung up and went back to pasting green leaves onto Katy's leotard, trying to thicken up the rather mangy-looking foliage.

It was well worth the effort, she thought to herself as she sat with David in the crowded school auditorium that night. Katy looked positively darling, a prominent part of Sherwood Forest, giving shelter to a small, freckle-faced Robin Hood. Of course, the trees did have a tendency to shift restlessly from foot to foot, making a rustling background noise that drowned out the speakers on occasion, and green leaves littered the stage as though it were a premature autumn—but, all in all, it was a brilliant performance, they assured Katy afterward.

Once back home, it took both of them to extricate her from the costume and scrub the green stage paint off her face and legs. Claire felt exhausted by the time they finally had her in bed. And she still had the kitchen to straighten up, she thought in dismay, since they'd only had time to bolt down supper before David arrived.

"Here, let me help you with that," he offered now, following Claire to the kitchen and seeing the counter littered with dishes.

"Thanks." She handed him a dishrag. "But I don't want to hear a word about my cooking!" she warned. Quite obviously they'd had fish sticks and macaroni and cheese for supper, the remains still in evidence on the dirty plates.

"Not a word," he vowed. "After the other night, I'm afraid I'm going to have to stop teasing you."

"It did turn out pretty well, didn't it?"

"I was impressed," he said, assuring her.

The meal she'd promised him had been a gourmet success. Naomi had come to her rescue with a simple, but elegant, recipe for baked halibut in a butter-and-lemon sauce. She'd made oven-browned potatoes and a salad with Naomi's special vinaigrette dressing and, for the pièce de résistance, she'd baked a chocolate cake that had been an instant hit with Katy.

"There's still cake left if you want some," she told David.

"Great!" David headed for the cupboard and got down plates, then he started the coffeemaker, moving around her kitchen familiarly while she finished loading the dishwasher, working together in companionable silence as if... as if they were an old married couple, Claire realized with a start. And as they sat together at the kitchen table, drinking coffee and eating cake, talking proudly of their daughter's performance, the feeling persisted. Tonight he'd managed to shake off the moodiness he'd had for the past few days since his talk with the Captain, and yet she had the feeling that that talk had left a lasting impression on him. She felt very close to David, tonight. They *fit,* somehow.

So when she walked with him to the door and he made to take her into his arms, she didn't hesitate for a moment. Everything about David seemed different tonight. The pressure of his lips against hers, of his hands on her back, felt different. They weren't insistently arousing, demanding a response—taking her response as his due.

Instead his mouth made erotically slow movements against her lips, waiting for her to yield, waiting patiently for *her* decision to prolong the contact. When she allowed his tongue to probe the soft, warm contours of her mouth, when she heard his moan of pleasure, she felt as though she'd been allowed to give a precious gift, willingly, instead of having it snatched from her.

The passion was still there, as always, but it was banked, guided and controlled, to warm slowly, instead of let loose to sear and burn like wildfire. Claire actually found herself taking the initiative, pressing her body closer to his, arching her back to bring her hips in contact with his.

The slow caress was building in intensity until Claire felt she would explode. She couldn't believe it when David gently pulled his mouth from hers and loosened his arms to make a small movement away.

"I think I'm starting to like this friend thing, after all," David said softly, with a shadow of a smile, his ragged breathing belying his light words. The smile faded as he stood looking down at her, her long, dark hair cascading around her shoulders, her almond-shaped green eyes staring up at him with bewildered desire.

"Claire, ask me to stay," he breathed.

Once again, he was giving her the choice. Forcing it to be her decision, not allowing her to blame a tide of passion for any loss of control. And, more than any other time in the past two years, Claire wanted desperately to say yes. It took all her willpower to force a small shake of her head.

She couldn't believe it when, with a final trail of a finger down her cheek, he left. Just like that. No teasing persuasion, no charming persistence. Only a tightening of features in a brief spasm of what she could almost call pain, a small smile good-night, that light touch on her cheek and then he was gone. Claire found herself, perversely, wishing he'd persisted as he usually did—wishing he'd insisted, demanded, cajoled.

Choosing to say no was proving infinitely more difficult than being *forced* to say no.

In the week to come Claire found herself in the unique position of actually having to look around for David. In the past it seemed as if he had always been underfoot, showing up at her door at inconvenient times, staying for a visit whenever he picked up or dropped off Katy, taking every opportunity to pursue his campaign for reconciliation. Now he appeared to have taken the Captain's comments very much to heart and was working feverishly on his book. As May approached the weather inched sluggishly toward spring, and David's open upper windows let the endless clicking of computer keys filter down to where Claire sat in her own study, with her own window open, clicking much more slowly on her own keyboard.

She was finding concentration difficult. Normally she felt very lucky to be able to work out of her home and, as was her nature, set herself strict, rigid office hours. But for some reason this past week often saw her leaving her desk and wandering through the house, staring into the refrigerator, watering the plants—and on one occasion, to her ever-lasting horror, she went so far as to watch a soap opera on the new television!

Claire's mind was straying again, unable to make sense of her last journal entry, the continuous tapping noise from above having a hypnotic effect that was making her sleepy even if it was only 9:30 a.m. She reached for her coffee cup and took a sip. Maybe she just needed another jolt of caffeine to get her blood pumping this morning. Cup in hand, she stood up and moved to the open window to poke her head out, breathing deeply of the crisp spring air.

It was no wonder she couldn't concentrate, she thought to herself, what with spring finally here and with everything so topsy-turvy, lately. First of all, there was David behaving so strangely—and the way she was reacting to him was definitely strange—and then there was the way everything had changed with Lawrence. She'd barely managed to sit through her obligatory evening out with him midweek to make up for their missed Friday, and had insisted on taking Katy along with them—something Katy had liked about as well as

Lawrence. And Claire found herself dreading to see 3:00 o'clock roll around today.

Her eyes happened to fall on her old van sitting in the driveway underneath the window. Maybe she and Katy could go for a long drive in the country this afternoon and just happen to conveniently be away from home at about 3:00. Of course, the poor old bug probably couldn't handle a long drive anywhere, the shape it was in. She really did need to give it an oil change and she had those new belts in the garage...

Claire looked back at the still-humming computer on her desk, its cursor blinking brightly off and on, begging for input. Then she turned to look once again at the sparkling spring morning and her ailing car sitting patiently below.

Click. The cursor faded from the screen with the punch of a button. And in less than ten minutes Claire had changed into the man-size pair of coveralls she kept hanging in the garage, had tugged a Minnesota Twins baseball cap onto her head, bill backward, and was lying on her back in the gravel under the rear engine.

She was so busy with the grease gun that she never noticed when David's keyboard was silenced. And she was cursing loudly enough trying to loosen the stubborn oil filter that she never heard the crunch of his shoes on the gravel. So his "Hi," coming just as the oil filter suddenly came free, startled her enough that she instinctively tried to sit up, banging her forehead against the rear axle.

"Damn it!" She shimmied out from under the van. "Don't *ever* sneak up on me like that!" She rubbed at the sore spot on her forehead, leaving a black smear of grease between her eyes.

"I wasn't sneaking," David protested. "Are you all right?"

"Yeah, I'm okay," Claire replied, regaining her equilibrium. "It's just a bump." She looked up at him from where she sat on the ground next to the van. "What are you up to? I've heard you working like a maniac on your story."

"I decided I deserved a break—and you look like you might need some help."

"Well..." Claire's expression was dubious. "I guess you could hand me stuff, if you want. It's a pain having to keep crawling out every time I need something."

David crouched down next to her. "Aren't you glad that I'm rich now and you don't have to do this for my car anymore? I can just pull into a garage whenever the new one needs work and say, 'Ring me when she's ready, old sport.'" David's imitation of an upper-crust Englishman had her giggling as she slid back under the engine.

"You know, this old bug's about on its last legs," David said, patting its rusted fender fondly. "You really should think about retiring her."

"Never!" Claire's voice was indignant. "She's got all new hoses and filters and I'm going to replace the belts today. She'll purr like a kitten when I'm done! Hand me a Phillips, would you? That's the one with the little star thingy on the end."

"I know what a Phillips screwdriver looks like, Claire," David said dryly. She heard him start to rummage noisily through her open toolbox.

"Sorry. I'm used to Katy helping me." Claire began to remove screws so she could take off the fan belt while she waited for the oil to drain from the engine. One screw was proving extremely difficult. She added more pressure, holding her breath while she exerted herself.

"Damn!" The screwdriver slipped, earning her a scraped and bleeding knuckle.

"Are you all right?" David asked again, bending down to peer under the car at her. "For the life of me, I can't understand why you like to do this!"

"I'm fine," she replied shortly. "But this screw's shot. I managed to mangle its head enough that it won't take a screwdriver." She slid out from under the engine and sat up, wiping her bleeding knuckle on a rag, her face mirroring her exasperation.

"*You* need a new car," David pronounced solemnly.

"Yeah, right! A new car!" she snorted. "Hey, you might be able to get me to buy a new TV, but don't try to reform me all at once."

"I mean it."

"So do I! I can't afford a new car!"

"Why not?"

"Why not?" she repeated, her voice incredulous, as if unable to believe he couldn't see the obvious. "Because of The Note!"

"What note?" David frowned, giving her a curious look.

"What note?" she said, parroting him, her face suddenly blank.

"You said 'Because of The Note.' You have a promissory note? I can't imagine you borrowing money."

"No. No, I don't. Of course not. I don't know what I was thinking of—why I said that—"

But Claire did know why—and she was shocked by what she'd said. The Note. It had always had capital letters in her mind as a child, whenever she heard her mother and father worrying over the words. The Note. As if it had a life of its own. She hadn't thought of it in years! Claire grabbed a wrench and disappeared back under the van, hiding her white face from David's too-interested eyes.

She had hated The Note. So many requests of her childhood had been turned down with the gentle, apologetic words, 'No, darling, The Note's due this month.' She hadn't had any idea what The Note was, but she'd vowed she'd never, ever have one of the horrible things that made it impossible for her to have the toys the other girls had. Years later she had realized the dreaded Note was merely a second mortgage her parents had taken out on the family home to cover her grandmother's lingering final illness. And, looking back, she knew that the entire repayment hadn't taken any more than five years—but those five years had seemed to be forever to a child. And The Note had assumed a permanent place in her subconscious.

Obviously a place important enough that it still reared its ugly head from time to time, Claire realized, pretending to loosen a bolt while her mind puzzled over the way those words had popped into her mouth. Lord, a psychiatrist would have a heyday with this one, she thought. Childhood insecurities shaping adult problem-solving, and all that. A psychiatrist would probably say she had this obsession with money, not because she didn't have it, but because her parents didn't have it when she was a child. A psychiatrist would probably say—

"Even *I* know you should be using a ratchet for that bolt." David's dry voice penetrated her speculation and she turned her head to see his face peering sideways at her, inches from the ground, holding out a ratchet.

"Oh. Right." Claire was flustered. "Thanks." She took the wrench from him. "But, you know, I think I'll just finish changing the oil and not worry about these belts right now, after all. I—I want to run an errand before Katy gets home from school."

"You can take my car, if you want," David offered.

"No, that's okay." Hurriedly she screwed on the new oil filter, crawled out from under the van and began adding fresh oil to the crankcase. David watched her quick efficient movements without comment, saying nothing when she peeled off the coveralls, tugged off the baseball cap, wiped her hands on a rag and got into the car to start the engine.

She checked for leaking oil then slammed the van door shut and started to put the engine into reverse to back out of the driveway. "Goodbye." She waved to him. "Thanks for the help."

"I'd think about washing my face, if I were you," he called after her, a smile struggling for release. Claire glanced in the rearview mirror and immediately stepped on the brake. She stared at the long black grease smudge on her forehead, right between her eyes, where she'd put her fingers to rub at the bump she'd gotten.

Bother! She turned off the engine and ran toward the apartment. By the time she'd washed and dragged a comb through her hair and got back out to the car, David had disappeared. The *click-click* of his word processor once again filled the air.

Chapter Eight

The drive to her parents house was accomplished in short order, traffic being light midmorning on a Friday. Claire made the drive on automatic pilot, stopping at red lights and shifting gears without being aware of it, passing familiar landmarks without notice. Her mind was busy dredging up everything she could remember about the dreaded Note, trying to think about it rationally, from an adult viewpoint, to force it to take its proper perspective in her subconscious. She didn't want a twenty-year-old memory to have such power over her! Rearing its ugly head every time she took out her checkbook!

Claire didn't really know why she had this sudden urge to visit her parents, to be in her childhood home. But maybe the well-loved surroundings would help her dispel this ghost that had unknowingly been haunting her all these years.

Home always looked the same, Claire thought with satisfaction as she pulled into the driveway of the old white house. It even smelled the same, she noticed when she pushed open the front door and entered the hallway. "Hi, it's me," she called out.

"In here." Her father's voice came from the living room where she found him reading the morning paper, leaning back comfortably in his favorite worn recliner.

"Where's Mom?" She dropped a kiss on her father's balding head then helped herself to the business section of the paper and dropped onto the floor next to his feet.

"Shower. She was out early doing something in the garden. You know how she is about spring and dirt. Can't leave the stuff alone."

Just then her mother came down the stairs, wrapped in an old pink robe, vigorously drying her hair with a towel. "Hello, sweetheart. I thought I heard your voice." She draped the towel over her shoulder. "What brings you out on a workday?"

Claire shrugged. "I've got a bad case of spring fever, I guess. Can't seem to concentrate."

"It *is* a lovely day. I planted two packages of lettuce and two of radishes and—"

"You hate radishes and so does Dad."

"I know, but I won't be able to plant tomatoes for ages and I just *had* to plant something! It's not like you can afford to buy vegetables in the store anymore."

Claire and her father exchanged indulgent smiles. But Claire's smile turned to a frown as she watched her mother tighten the belt on her robe.

"Mom, what are you still doing in that ratty old pink thing? I gave you a new one for Christmas."

"I know you did, and it's perfectly lovely—but I put that up for something special. In case I have to go to the hospital or something. You never know."

"But you put up the robe I gave you the year before that for special, too!" Claire fretted. "You were supposed to *wear* this year's!"

"But if I wear it, it won't be new anymore and will end up looking just like this one." Her mother's voice had the overly reasonable tone one used when explaining things to a worrisome child.

Claire opened her mouth to protest further, but her mother held up a quieting hand. "This robe is just fine—it's comfortable and I like knowing those nice ones are there if I need them someday."

Again Claire and her father exchanged glances. They both knew it was pointless to continue the discussion. Someday Claire was just going to go into her mother's room, kidnap that old pink thing and turn it into a grease rag!

Her mother had gone to stand in front of a framed mirror that decorated a portion of one wall. She was running her fingers through her short hair, fluffing it dry. "I wonder if I can get your aunt Ruth to come over and give me a perm this week," she mused, studying her reflection.

"Now, Mom, you know all those chemicals make her break out."

"I know, but—" She caught her daughter's eye in the mirror. "I don't suppose you'd feel like giving it a try?"

"No, thanks! Why don't you just go to the shop like everyone else?"

"And pay fifty dollars for something that's going to grow out and get cut off in a month? Heaven's no!" She turned to look more closely at Claire. "Are you feeling all right, darling? You look a little peaked."

"I'm okay. Maybe a tiny headache is all. I bumped my head on the axle when I was changing the oil this morning."

"Mmm. You look a little gray around the eyes. You used to get like that when you were small and were starting a fever." Instinctively she walked toward Claire, her hand held out in the age-old maternal gesture to place a palm on Claire's forehead.

Claire managed to dodge just in time. "I don't have a fever!"

"All right, all right. I just worry about you, that's all. You work too hard and wear yourself out. And Lord knows, a person can't afford to get sick these days, what with the cost of doctors and medicine— and our insurance premiums! Darling, you wouldn't believe..."

Claire had stopped listening. The cost of vegetables. The cost of a permanent. The cost of medicine. Her mind turned inwardly, remembering other conversations.

I like that blouse, Mom.

It's nice isn't it? It was only $7.99 at the Discount Mart.

Chicken for supper again, Mom?

It was on sale this week. The price of beef has gone through the roof. I think they want us all to be vegetarians, or something!

I tried to call but your phone was busy.

We checked on getting a private line, but you wouldn't believe what they want to charge for the privilege of talking!

Example after example, like a stuck record, played through Claire's brain. How had she never noticed before the way her mother broke everything down to the level of cost? Was her mother really so price conscious? Being her parents' accountant, Claire knew they were financially secure—not wealthy, but they would be comfortable for the rest of their lives. And yet her mother still seemed to worry continually about the cost of things. Good grief, how much money would it take before she felt secure?

Claire's spinning thoughts were pulled up short. How much money would she, herself, need before *she* felt secure. Before she felt she could afford a new television—or a new car? Was this some family legacy passed down from mother to daughter? She worried about money because her mother worried about money? And would Katy carry on the family tradition?

"Claire, you really are looking pale." Her mother's concerned voice brought her back. "How bad did you bump your head, anyway?"

"Just a tap, nothing much." Claire got to her feet. "But, look, I better get going. I just wanted to say hi and take a little break from work. Katy will be getting off the bus soon."

On the drive home, Claire tried to look at herself objectively. She really wasn't as bad as her mother, she protested. She really wasn't. Good Lord, the woman wore the same robe year after year while two brand-new ones, still in tissue paper, sat stacked neatly in their gift boxes on a closet shelf. Claire would never—

She brought the car to a halt in her driveway and turned off the key, staring blindly out the windshield. Minutes passed. Then Claire flung open the door and fairly ran into the apartment, into her bedroom, and began rummaging through a bottom dresser drawer. There it was. She pulled out a cashmere sweater, cream colored and baby soft.

Quickly she found a pair of nail clippers in her nightstand and used them to clip off the tags still attached to the sweater with little strands of plastic. Then she stripped off her sweatshirt and pulled the sweater over her head—the first time she'd had it on since the Christmas David had given it to her five years before.

Claire heard the sound of Katy opening the front door. "Don't take off your coat," she called. Claire met her daughter at the door dressed in jeans, tennis shoes and a cashmere sweater, and turned her around to usher her back outside.

"Where are we going?" Katy asked, staring up at her mother in surprise.

"I don't know yet," Claire replied grimly. "But wherever it is, we're going to spend some money."

* * *

Claire didn't have to invent some excuse not to see Lawrence when he called that afternoon, after all. Her head had begun to ache in earnest by then and she told him she planned on spending a quiet evening at home with a book and some aspirin.

"I must have hit my head harder than I thought," she'd explained to him.

"I hope you aren't coming down with something," Lawrence had suggested darkly. "You probably picked up some bug at Katy's play last week, jammed into that stuffy old auditorium with all those kids."

Claire had assured him she'd feel fine after a good night's sleep and hung up, not wanting to question why she felt so relieved.

She spent the rest of the evening playing with Katy and catching up on household chores, vaguely restless and out of sorts—and feeling definitely overdressed every time she caught sight of her cashmere sweater and newly manicured nails gleaming with Passion's Pink Promise. She and Katy had spent the afternoon at the beauty salon getting their hair done, and Claire had gone so far as to have a manicure and—something she'd never had before in her life, considering it a totally decadent waste of money—a pedicure.

Now she pattered around the apartment in bare feet, Passion's Pink Promise toes winking like jewels in the carpet, wishing she didn't feel so achy—and wishing that David would stop by. All dressed up with nowhere to go, she thought morosely, with only a five-year-old to appreciate her freshly styled hair that wouldn't be fresh in the morning. And passion, as it had a way of doing, had already started to chip while she was washing the dishes.

Sighing, Claire took two aspirin and went to bed.

She didn't get a good night's sleep, after all. The aspirin didn't help her headache and sometime during the night her throat began to get scratchy. It looked as though Lawrence was right—she had caught something at Katy's play.

Thankfully Katy didn't seem to have come down with it yet, Claire thought as they sat on the floor by the big bay window in the living room, a checkerboard lying between them. Her head was hurting enough to make concentration difficult and she was almost ready to tell Katy she could go ahead and spend the morning watching cartoons after all.

"King me!" Katy crowed suddenly, loud enough to make Claire wince.

"Shh!" Claire glanced down at the board. Sure enough, one of Katy's black checkers had managed to make it all the way across the red and black squares. Well, it didn't look as though she was going to have to pretend to lose this game! Obediently she balanced a second black disk on top of the invading checker. "There. You're kinged. And I'm tired. Why don't you turn on the TV and I'll just sit here and read for a while, okay?"

With a whoop of delight, Katy ran for the remote control. Claire managed to lift her aching body up off the floor and settle in the chair next to the window. She picked up her book from the end table and squinted at the page, the morning sunlight reflected off its whiteness and made her eyes sting and water.

"Katy, pull the drapes for me, will you?" But Katy was engrossed in a commercial for a sugar-laden superhero cereal even Claire would never consider buying. So she struggled to the window, stooping slightly with shoulders curved inward as if trying to make a smaller target for the pain. She fumbled for the cord, hidden in the folds of the curtains, when a sudden movement in front of her made her let out a startled squeal.

"Good Lord, you scared me to death!" she gasped, leaning closer to look through the screen of the open window. David was standing directly underneath, squeezed among the arborvitaes, an old aluminum ladder in hand, his head on level with her stomach.

"Are you making a habit of sneaking up on me?" she demanded. Her hand went to the small spot on her forehead that had turned an unbecoming shade of greenish-purple, a result of David's sneak attack yesterday.

"You're just too jumpy lately. I wasn't being exactly quiet." David shoved the ladder against the house, making a horrible scraping sound where it touched the siding, doing excruciating things to the nerve endings on Claire's scalp. He looked up at her with a "see what I mean?" expression on his face. "Hey, I like your hair."

"Thanks." Claire was pleased he'd noticed the new fringe of bangs. The woman at the salon had sworn they'd make Claire look five years younger—and hide the bruise. "I had it done yesterday. And a manicure.'' She held lacquer-tipped fingernails down at the bottom of the window for his inspection.

But David didn't seem too impressed. In fact, his eyes had narrowed and his lips were disapprovingly firm. ''All fancied up for the old Friday bowling night with Lawrence, huh?''

''As a matter of fact, no. I didn't go out with Lawrence last night. I was sick—am sick. I think I've caught a cold.''

''Hmm, you do look a little gray around the eyes.'' He peered up at her. ''You always get gray like that whenever you get a fever—''

''I know, I know. I've been to Mother's.'' Claire pressed her nose against the screen and tried to look down at the material David had piled on the ground by his feet.

''What are you doing?'' Those boxes looked like the ones from the garage—those old tubes of— It couldn't be! ''You're going to—''

''Yup!'' He gave a determined nod. ''I'm going to caulk these downstairs windows.''

Claire managed to bite back the ''You're kidding!'' that sprang to her lips. Instead, she watched in silence as he awkwardly inserted a new tube of caulk into the metal dispensing gun he held in his hand, and she had to grit her teeth to keep from telling him to—

Ahh. There. He saw it for himself. Unflustered, he calmly removed the tube and picked up a utility knife, cutting the sealed plastic tip of the tube straight across to allow the caulk to come out. Then he reinserted the tube, climbed up a couple of rungs of the ladder, held the tip of the gun against the edge of the window and began to squeeze the handle. Claire couldn't see the resulting line of caulk, but from David's concerned expression she could imagine the wavy globs.

She couldn't help herself. "If you cut the tip on an angle, you'll get a finer bead. It's easier to control that way."

David gave her a look that made Claire shrug her shoulders and give a small, helpless smile. He climbed back down the ladder and recut the opening. There. Much better. She could tell by the way his arm moved in a smooth stroke down the edge of the window frame.

"You don't have to do this, you know," she told him after watching him for several minutes, squinting in the sunlight. "I mean, it's not your house. It's not your problem anymore. You don't have to do stuff like this anymore."

"It's not my house," he agreed, not turning his head, concentrating fiercely on his task, "but it's my daughter sitting in front of this drafty old window. And how do I know you didn't catch your cold from some chill air leaking around this very window?" He paused, lowering the caulk, and stood back a foot to consider his handiwork. He looked satisfied.

"I've been meaning to do this for—I don't know how long."

"For years."

"Yeah, for years. Thought I better finally get to it before I leave."

"Leave?" Claire blamed the croaky way it came out on her sore throat.

David nodded, heaving the ladder to the other side of the window, trying to maneuver through the thick shrubbery. "Barney called last night," he grunted. "He's arranged a four-city tour for *The Green of Spring*. I leave Wednesday for New York, then hit Boston, Philadelphia and Washington. Autographing parties and receptions and all that." He said it with an attempt at nonchalance, but couldn't hide the pleased, proud smile that curved his mouth.

"Hey, congratulations! I know you love that sort of thing. You'll have a great time." He was looking so cocky that she hated to burst his bubble, but—

"David?"

"Hmm?" He turned to look where she was pointing, "Damn! Damn!" The caulk gun he'd laid on top of a bush while he moved the ladder was busily oozing itself dry, decorating the green shrubbery with long strands of white. He hadn't snapped the button to relieve the pressure before he'd put it down.

"Push in on the end! Push! Push!" She couldn't control her giggles as he grabbed the gun and began to fumble with the unfamiliar tool. Her laughter triggered a cough and she stood alternately laughing and coughing, both making her head ache worse than ever.

David glared up at her, his eyes sparkling with suppressed laughter as he tried to look fierce, white goo covering his hands and dripping down to his jeans. "Why don't you go to bed?" he growled. "You're sick, remember!"

Later, lying in bed, Katy coloring at the foot of it, Claire listened to David moving around outside. She liked hearing the sound of the ladder, his footsteps, his humming. It was really sweet of him to do that, she thought, especially since carpentry-type work was certainly not his forte. And to worry about them catching cold? Very considerate. It was nice to have a man around the house, she thought drowsily. And as awful as she felt, what with her achiness and her head and her throat—with David just outside she really did feel a little better.

The buzzing doorbell woke her and she struggled to sit up through a haze of sleep, feeling worse, if that were possible, than when she and Katy had laid down to take a nap after lunch. She glanced at the clock— 2:30. She'd only slept an hour, not long enough to account for the heavy, drugged sensation that weighed down her limbs and made it difficult to move toward the door. She really had one hell of a cold, she thought miserably, her groggy mind indulging in a moment of self-pity.

And to see Lawrence standing on her doorstep increased the self-pity tenfold.

"Claire! You look awful!" Lawrence sounded shocked at the sight of her.

She didn't care. "You woke me up." She stumbled to the kitchen and tore off a section of paper towel, using it to blow her nose on. "I told you I was sick."

"I know, darling, but I never imagined you were this sick." He followed her into the kitchen and stood helplessly, staring at her. "You should be in bed."

"I *was* in bed!" Claire sounded grieved. "I told you, you woke me up."

"I shouldn't have come, I'm sorry. But I was worried about you. You've been so—so different lately, so distant—canceling two Friday nights in a row. Well, I thought—"

"You thought I was faking it?"

Lawrence's face flushed guiltily. But Claire could see he was genuinely concerned about her and by now she had woken up enough to forgive him.

"It's all right." She blew her nose again. "I could use a little company. It will keep me from thinking about how rotten I feel."

"Let's go sit down on the couch. You can rest." He started to lead her toward the living room, then paused, his hand solicitously on her elbow. "Can I get you something? Maybe some hot tea with honey and lemon?"

"That would be wonderful," Claire said gratefully, ready to be pampered. "I don't have any lemon—but honey's in the cupboard next to the sink. And the tea bags are in the coffee canister."

"Right. You go sit down and I'll make you a nice cup of tea."

That was kind of him, Claire thought, snuggling back against a sofa pillow and pulling up her knees, tucking her robe around her bare feet. So why did she feel so irritated to hear cupboard doors banging as he opened door after door, searching for the cups, the saucers, the spoons. David knew right where everything was. She found herself gritting her teeth and had to keep from barging into the kitchen to make the tea herself. Finally, some minutes later, Lawrence proudly came in bearing a cup of tea as if it were a gift offering to the gods. He rattled it down onto the coffee table, sloshing a good bit of hot liquid into the saucer.

"There." His sigh of relief let her know what a chore it had been for him. He settled himself next to her, giving the habitual tug at his trouser legs as he sat down. "Now you just relax. Really, this gives us a chance to talk." He turned to face her. "I've been wanting to talk to you about our little discussion of a while back."

Oh, no! Not now! Claire moaned silently. I'm too sick. I can't handle this.

"Have you had a chance to think any more about it?" Lawrence took her hand, his dark eyes appealing. "I know I promised not to rush you but it's been several weeks now and we haven't really discussed it again since that night. I thought maybe now . . . ?"

He was so earnest, so serious. He really is a kind man, Claire thought unhappily—just as he's always been. It's not his fault that the way he tugged at his trouser legs set her teeth on edge now—he'd done that since the first day she met him. But now, now it annoyed her.

"Things have been so hectic lately," Claire mumbled, "work and everything. . . ." She didn't want to meet his eyes. It wasn't his fault. It was she that had changed, not him.

"Of course they have," Lawrence sympathized, patting her hand. "And now probably isn't the right time for this, either, but—" He reached into the pocket of his jacket and pulled out a small ring box.

Oh, no!

Lawrence snapped open the lid and held out the box to her, but Claire could only gaze at the engagement ring, its large pearl milky white, nestled in a circle of glittering diamonds. She made no move to take it. Still Lawrence held it out, flat on his palm, waiting in his quiet way for her decision, offering, asking—

Finally Claire raised stricken eyes to meet his. Her throat ached as much from unshed tears, now, as from her cold.

"I understand." Lawrence closed his hand over the box, shutting it with a muffled snap and dropped it back into his pocket. "I was hoping you were finally over him. For a while there, it seemed like you were ready."

"Ready?" Claire repeated weakly, not wanting to understand.

Lawrence's smile was sad, gentle. "It's all right. I know you still love David."

Claire wanted to deny it—vehemently. But she couldn't. She couldn't force herself to say the words. Not to this man who really did know her quite well and who sat there so patiently, kindly, facing a truth painful to him while only wanting the best for her.

"I...I..." Her lips trembled.

"But I want you to know that I still want to marry you all the same," he went on. "I don't care about David. I love you and Katy and I think we could be happy together. I know how you feel. After Barbara died I thought I could never get over it, but you really do learn to love again. And I want to be there, waiting for you, when you're ready for me."

Tears were rolling down Claire's cheeks now. How could she still love David? After everything? After two years, how could her traitorous heart still love him? While Lawrence, Lawrence was kind and successful and . . . and kind—and she didn't love him.

"I'm sorry," Claire told him. "I can't."

"I can wait," he told her hopefully. "I'm a patient man."

But she shook her head, swallowing around the lump in her throat. "I don't think time is the answer. In fact—well, David has been talking about trying again for quite a while now and, well—"

"It won't work, Claire! It never does!" His tone was unhappy yet uncritical. He was plainly hurt, but he had no desire to be hurtful in return.

"Lawrence, he's changed! No, *I've* changed. I've had to rethink some old attitudes and perceptions and—" She waved a hand dismissingly, impatient with explanations. "Anyway, we're different people now, and I think we have a chance this time." It was important to her that he understood. Or maybe that she understood.

And Lawrence, gentleman to the end, wished them both luck and happiness, promised to be there for her if she ever needed him, kissed her goodbye and showed himself out so she wouldn't have to get up from her warm spot on the couch.

Claire wrapped her arms around her raised knees and cradled her aching head against them. She was sick. She was in love with her ex-husband. She was crazy!

The sound of her front door opening and light footsteps approaching forced her to look up.

"Hi! What was the old king of office supplies doing here on a *Saturday?* Did he lose his appointment book? Don't tell me he actually did something spontaneous for once!"

"Go away," Claire groaned. Love or not, she couldn't take anymore.

Chapter Nine

"Go away? What? And leave you all alone?"

Claire nodded. "That sounds just wonderful," she sniffled. "All alone."

But, naturally, that didn't stop David from joining her on the couch. "I wanted to make sure you didn't need anything. Chicken soup? A humidifier? Aspirin?"

Claire shook her head after each question. All she wanted was to go back and join Katy in the bedroom and sleep. She needed rest, quiet—and time to think. And she didn't like the way David was peering at her. She knew she looked awful!

She really did look ill, David was thinking sympathetically, but there was something else . . . He studied her face carefully. Her eyes seemed to be overbright and red-rimmed from more than a cold—as though she'd been crying—

"Did Lawrence say something to upset you?" he asked suspiciously.

Again Claire shook her head, but David caught the way she quickly averted her eyes, suddenly intent on staring at his shirtfront.

Hmm, David thought to himself. Mr. Punctuality comes on a day other than a Friday, Claire's been crying, the old goat leaves looking even glummer than usual... David's blue eyes narrowed as he silently added up the evidence.

He had it! "You turned him down!" he shouted triumphantly.

"It's none of your business!" Claire tried for haughtiness.

But David was whooping and slapping his leg. "That's it, isn't it? You told him to take a hike!" He was grinning from ear to ear.

"There's nothing funny about hurting somebody you care about and who cares about you!"

David sobered immediately. "You're right. I'm sorry." He didn't look that sorry. "But I can't pretend I'm not happy you told him no. Bigamy's against the law, you know, and marrying him would definitely be an obstacle in our relationship, Claire."

She managed a weak smile and picked up her cup to finish the rest of her tea, but her throat was too sore to drink. Grimacing with pain, she began to dig around in the pocket of her robe for a tissue and gave David a croak of thanks when he handed her the box from the coffee table. She blew her nose vigorously.

David frowned. "Damn! I hate the thought of being out of town when you're this sick. I just talked to Barney and he wants to move the book tour up a couple of days. Now I'm supposed to leave on Monday—"

"Don't worry about me. Mom's always there if I need anything."

"And I guess I can ask Naomi to keep an eye on you, too."

"Sure. I'll be fine. I just need some sleep," Claire hinted pointedly.

"All the same, *I'd* feel better waiting till *you* were better. Maybe I'll give Barney a call back, see if we can't juggle the schedule a little more." David sighed. "My long-distance bill is getting to be astronomical. It'd probably cost less in the long run to move to New York."

Claire felt her stomach flip-flop. "I was wondering about that just the other day," she said, attempting nonchalance. "Whether or not you were thinking about moving someplace a little fancier—now that you're rich and famous. Minnesota's not exactly the publishing capital of the country."

"Maybe not, but I'd have to be crazy to move," David replied lightly. "I've got the best of both worlds right here. I mean, I've got a wife and child under my roof without all the demands of a husband or father. What man could ask for more?"

Claire couldn't believe she'd heard right. Her breath caught in her throat and her eyes flew to his. David looked as shocked as she felt and where her face quickly lost what little color it had, his cheeks began to stain a dull red. An uncomfortable silence grew between them as they stared at each other, both realizing just how true his words were—even if he had meant them as a joke.

It was no joke to Claire. She was the first to break the silence. "We've made divorce pretty convenient for you, haven't we?" She was unable to keep the bitterness from coloring her voice.

"Claire, I didn't mean it like that! I—"

But Claire had been hurt to the quick by his casual words. Unknowingly David had touched a raw nerve, a canker that had been festering inside her heart for two years. *She* might have been the one who kicked him out that night—but *he* was the one who left! And who stayed away! Of course she'd been angry about the new car, blazingly angry, but she'd never considered for a moment that he'd actually stay away, stay upstairs, allow a fight to turn into a divorce.

"I always wondered why you didn't come back down the next morning...why you didn't try to stop me filing for divorce."

"Stop you?" David sounded incredulous. "You were at your lawyers by nine o'clock that morning and he'd filed the papers by noon!"

You could have come down at eight o'clock then! she wanted to cry out. You could have fought harder for me—for us! But she didn't. Because now she knew why he'd let her have her way. The best of both worlds, he'd said. And she supposed it was—for someone as immature and self-centered as David!

"Hey, now! Don't look at me like that!" David ordered, angry and hurt by the condemnation on her face. "You know damn well I tried and tried to talk to you but you shut me out every time. Making like you were so self-sufficient that you and Katy didn't need me—"

"Would it have mattered if we did need you?" Claire shot back. "You were never there for us!"

"You never *let* me be there for you! If *you* weren't in control you didn't feel safe! You had every second of our lives planned, mapped out, neat little diagrams of living—hell, what did you need me for?"

Well! She wasn't about to listen to any more of this! Claire struggled to her feet, wishing she didn't feel so dizzy so she could sweep out of the room with the disdain the situation warranted. As it was she swayed so unsteadily that David instinctively jumped up and reached out to grab her arm.

But she flinched away before he could touch her, trying to focus enough to give him a chilly stare. Good Lord, she must have been delirious to tell Lawrence she was thinking of reconciling with this man, that he had changed! Love him she might, but a life with David was still out of the question. *Nothing* had changed!

"Nothing's changed," she muttered aloud, trying to pull her robe tighter around her. "And why is it so damn bright in here?" she demanded angrily, squinting toward the table lamp whose soft glow was stabbing into her eyes like daggers. Claire moved forward, hand outstretched toward the offending light, but her unresponsive feet stumbled into David.

This time he did grab her, and he immediately let out a worried oath as the heat of her feverish body seared through the thin material of her robe and scorched his hand where it touched her. He pressed his other palm quickly to her cheek.

"My God, you're burning up!" A strong arm was immediately under her knees, lifting her, cradling her into a broad, familiar chest, carrying her toward her bedroom.

"Put me down!" Claire ordered—or tried to order. But the words wouldn't form, and it was her last coherent thought until morning.

Her head ached, her nose was stuffed up, the damned light still hurt her half-open eyes—and now she itched. Everywhere. Claire lifted a hand and tried to reach a particularly annoying spot on her shoulder blade, only to find her hand grasped and pulled firmly away. She tried to open her sleepy eyes wider, to ask whoever it was to scratch her back for her because now that she was waking up the itching was starting to drive her crazy.

"Don't scratch." It was David's voice. "You'll just make it worse and end up with scars."

Scars! That brought her fully awake. She scrambled into a sitting position against the pillows, glancing wildly around her bedroom to orient herself, yanking down the covers from around her chin and searching frantically over her arms. Red spots! She kicked her legs free of the blankets. More red spots!

"*No!* I've had the chicken pox. I *know* I've had the chicken pox."

"Nope. You had the measles. I've already checked with your mother."

"Katy!"

"Should come down with them anytime now," David assured her cheerfully, tucking her legs back under the sheet and straightening the covers over her.

Claire didn't resist. She sank back against the pillows, too weak to hold her head up any longer now that the rush of adrenaline had left her. "It was the school play, wasn't it?"

"Probably so. I imagine we were sitting in a positive hotbed of chicken-pox virus in that auditorium."

"You okay?"

"Had them when I was a couple of months old, it seems. I already called my mother, too."

Claire nodded and closed her eyes. She couldn't keep them open. She couldn't believe how weak she was. How was she going to manage when Katy got sick, too! She struggled to speak, her words coming out a whisper. "Mom—"

"What?" David leaned forward to hear.

"Call Mom," Claire repeated. "She'll know what to do. She'll take care of us—me and Katy."

"Don't worry," David soothed, a shadow of pain passing over his features at her words. "Don't worry. You just rest now. Go back to sleep."

She was so tired. She tried to lick her dry lips but her mouth was full of dusty cotton, her tongue thick. She felt a cup pressed to her lips and David's voice, coming from a long way away, urged her to drink, holding the cup steady while she struggled to sip the juice. Ahh, that was better.

She heard David's voice a lot that day, always from a great distance, echoing down a tunnel. He was continually trying to get her to swallow something—either pills or juice—when all she wanted to do was sleep. She was vaguely aware when Katy joined her in bed that evening, cuddling close and complaining miserably that she didn't feel good, her temperature already on its way up. Claire's maternal instincts, primordially strong even when desperately ill herself, tried to force her fevered mind alert enough to help her child, but once again David's voice was there, calming her, urging her to rest, reassuring her that everything was fine—Katy was fine—she was fine—just sleep now....

And she slept until the following morning. Even semiconscious as she'd been, her internal body clock had continued to tick and she was now aware that it was Monday evening and that she'd been in bed since Saturday afternoon. She laid still with her eyes closed, letting her senses one by one bring the world back into focus. She knew it was Monday—and that something was supposed to happen on Monday... something... no, she couldn't get her fuzzy thoughts to sharpen; she let the niggling worry slip away.

Sounds filtered through to her. She could hear the clink of the metal chain on the paper boy's bike as he passed by on the sidewalk, the thump as the newspaper landed on target against the front door. She could hear the radio coming from the kitchen, accompanied by the smell of supper cooking. Rosemary. David always put it in his stew. A light breeze touched her face; the window must be open, bringing in cool spring air to freshen the room.

Now Claire took a physical inventory. Her head? Not aching so badly, thank God. She tried to swallow. All right, not so sore. But the itching—damn, there it was, starting to build the more awake she became. Unable to stop herself, she shrugged her shoulders, moving them up and down against the sheets, trying to find some relief from the itching. The rhythmic squeaking of the rocking chair next to her bed stopped at her movements. Good. Mother was here, just as she had been when she was sick as a child, rocking by her bedside while she slept.

"Momma?" she asked in a rusty voice, trying to open heavy eyes.

"I'm here, Claire." It was David. "Stop wiggling around like that. It's not going to help a bit."

"But it itches," she protested feebly, squinting over at him. He looked terrible, she thought. Even in the semidarkened room, lines of tiredness were visible around his mouth and eyes.

"I know it itches. And I've got some pink stuff here that's supposed to help. Do you want me to put some on you?"

"I want a shower," she said testily. "And you look like you need a nap—and a shave. You're a mess." Claire made as if to push aside the covers and sit up. But, somehow, her body wasn't going along with it at all. Her head wouldn't lift from the pillow and her hands did no more than pluck at the suddenly heavy comforter. "Well? Aren't you going to help me?"

"Nope." David grinned at her, sending up a tired prayer of thanks that her fever had finally broken and the glazed look had left her eyes. And he was heartily relieved that it didn't look as though he was going to have a battle keeping her in bed. She obviously wasn't going anywhere soon.

"David!"

He shook his head firmly. "A sponge bath only for tonight."

Knowing she was in no position to argue, Claire gave in. It was too tiring to insist, anyway. "Okay. Could you ask Mother to come in here, then, and help me with it?"

"Your mother's not here," David told her.

"She's not?"

"But she stopped by this afternoon and left the pink stuff for the itching."

"Oh." Claire was surprised. She'd taken it for granted that her mother would come over and take charge of nursing her and Katy.

"Let me gather together a few supplies and I'll sponge you down."

Claire frowned. He made it sound rather like hosing out the garage. "Never mind. I'll wait and take a shower in the morning. Don't bother."

"It's no bother. You'll feel fresher and you'll sleep better tonight." He got to his feet and started for the door. "I'll be right back. You just wait here."

As if she was going anywhere! Claire thought in disgust. Just waking up had made her tired. She found herself dozing off again before David had even returned. It took the soothing warmth of a wet cloth moving up and down her arm to wake her up again. The cloth moved over the other arm, her hands, around her neck and face, a thick towel drying her off

immediately after so she wouldn't chill. She felt the
covers being pulled down to the foot of the bed and
heard the sound of the cloth being wrung out in a pan
of water before it started over her legs and feet. It
moved up her leg as high as the hem of her nightshirt,
then paused, seemingly unsure how, or if, to continue.

Claire shifted slightly, opening her eyes. "Umm,
maybe you could put on some of that itching medicine now?"

"Right." David's voice sounded strange, tight.
"Sure."

From the way she felt, the majority of the sores
seemed to be on her back, or at least that's where the
itching was the most concentrated. But there were
some on her legs and arms, and it definitely felt as if
there was one smack in the middle of her chin. She had
no desire to look in a mirror whatsoever.

"Can you sit up?" David asked, lifting under her
arms to move her up against the pillows. She reached
behind her, and with his help, managed to pull and tug
the back of the nightshirt up until the majority of her
back was exposed to his ministration. Claire tried not
to think about the fact that the T-shirt she had on now
was not the one that she was wearing on Saturday afternoon. Better not to ask how or who.

David picked up the plastic bottle from the nightstand and shook it a few times, then poured some of
the lotion on a cotton ball and began to dab it on her
back. Ahh. That felt wonderful! From the number of
times he tilted the bottle Claire could imagine how
many sores there must be. Her back was literally

painted pink by the time he was finished. He did the same for most of the rest of her body, although she quite firmly told him she could manage a few areas without his help. That he didn't have some saucy comeback to that was proof of how tired he was.

"Thanks." Her appreciation was heartfelt, the itching had subsided. Poor David looked ragged. And no wonder, playing nursemaid to both her and Katy! "How's Katy?" Claire asked. "She always hates staying in bed, and I bet the itching's driving her crazy."

"She's doing okay. She's in the kitchen eating supper."

"The kitchen!" Claire exclaimed disapprovingly. "Is she up to that?" She couldn't even contemplate getting out of bed, let alone being up and around eating supper!

"Now, now, don't go all mother hen on me." David's tone was calming. "It looks like she's got a pretty light case. Her fever's gone already and the itching's not that bad since she's only got four spots."

"Four!"

"When I called the doctor he said that chicken pox can be mild in young kids—it's adult cases that get complicated. He said you'll probably be in bed for a couple weeks and—"

"A couple weeks! I can't lay around for—"

"I told him you'd say that." David laughed. "But he said I wouldn't have to worry about keeping you in bed—you're going to feel awful for quite a while yet."

"Well, don't sound so happy about it," Claire grumbled, letting David help settle her back down under the covers.

"Anything else you need right now?" he asked solicitously, pulling the comforter up to her chin. "I want to put fresh sheets on Katy's bed while she's eating and then get a load of laundry started."

"Wait a minute! You shouldn't be doing all this. I'm sure Mom can come over and help out. You don't need to—"

"Go back to sleep," David interrupted, his voice firm.

"Wait!" He'd started toward the door and was pulling it shut behind him. "I'm not really sleepy anymore. Why don't you send Katy in when she's through eating and I'll entertain her for the rest of the evening. Then maybe you can get some sleep yourself."

"It's a deal."

A few minutes later Katy came slowly into the room, dressed in her pajamas, carefully balancing a bowl of stew on a tray for Claire. After Katy had proudly displayed her four spots and inspected with great interest Claire's hundreds, she spread out her collection of ponies on the bed and Claire helped her comb brightly colored manes and tails for the rest of the evening. They fell asleep together, two dark heads sharing the same pillow, a rainbow jumble of horses at their feet.

Claire had never slept so much in her life! It appeared the doctor had been right—she was going to spend two weeks in bed. A week had already passed and Claire was barely managing to sit up an hour or two a day. The rest of the time she slept, occasionally read—and mostly thought.

Nothing like a week or two flat on your back without the energy to put your feet on the floor to give a person a chance to do some heavy thinking, she told herself sourly one morning when the itching had been particularly bad. Time to think about the scheme of things, so to speak. Such as how the world seemed to be going along perfectly well without her attention. Claire had been positively, and uncomfortably, shocked to discover that she wasn't after all, indispensable.

By the end of the week Katy had been ready to return to school and every morning she was fed, dressed, hair combed and on the bus without Claire having moved from her bed. Meals were cooked, laundry folded, homework done—neither her house nor her child seemed to be missing her personal ministrations in the least. Her clients hadn't revolted and left her for other accountants, nor had they gone into bankruptcy while she slept.

It was definitely a sobering, somewhat humbling experience, and Claire wasn't sure she liked it one little bit.

Restlessly she kicked off the restricting sheets and rolled over onto her stomach to stare out the window, bunching her pillow into a ball and resting her chin on it. She wasn't used to not being needed! How could things be going along so smoothly without her! Could it be that—perhaps—what she'd always prided her-

self on as her maturity and reliability, her levelhead-
edness, had in fact covered a hint—just a hint—of
insecurity? Could her want—*need*—to plan and organize and schedule be just a tad compulsive? Could
it possibly reflect a fear in her own abilities to cope?
Could David—oh, it was a horrifying thought!—could
he have been right when he'd accused her of needing
a diagram to live by?

Claire gritted her teeth as much from her thoughts
as to keep from scratching and reached for the bottle
on the nightstand to dab more pink lotion on her skin.
She was already on her third bottle of the stuff. She
was starting to hate the very smell of it.

David. Her thoughts centered on him as she sat up
in bed, waiting for the pink blobs to dry before she laid
back down. Once again, their relationship was going
through a strange metamorphosis. David, flighty, fun-
loving, totally unpredictable David, was taking charge
of her life, being strong and capable, while Claire,
dependable, reliable Claire, was lying in bed as weak
as a baby. This was a complete reversal of how Claire
perceived their "roles" and she was surprised at how
much it disturbed her.

She was used to depending on herself and, if worse
came to worst, her parents were always ready to lend
a helping hand. But this last week, although her
mother had stopped by daily, bringing casseroles and
Vitamin C filled oranges by the dozen, it was David
who was constantly there when she needed something. If he wasn't actually in the room with her she
knew he was within hailing distance. She could hear
him talking quietly with Katy in the living room in the

evenings and was comforted by the sound of him moving around the apartment.

She wouldn't have been able to make it through this without David. He'd rescheduled her clients, picked up her clothes from the cleaners, canceled Katy's gymnastics lesson and got her missed assignments from school—all without a word of prompting from Claire. She found herself actually *relying* on David. Now that was a startling revelation!

Of course, in theory, she was still supposed to be mad at him, she supposed. Neither of them had referred to the fight they'd had the afternoon she'd collapsed. Her illness and his nursing had somehow preempted the normal period of coolness following such a heated argument. By some unspoken agreement they both acted as if it had never happened. But still Claire couldn't help thinking about it.

She remembered her angry, feverish words and was embarrassed. How could she have said he was never there for her? He was being the best friend a woman could have—and at a cost to himself, too. Claire knew that caring for her and Katy was taking him away from his writing. He'd appropriated her office computer and she could hear him typing away late at night when he thought she was asleep. In fact, guilt had prompted her to start going to bed when Katy did, feigning a sleepiness she didn't feel, in order to give him a few extra hours on his book so that he could get to bed himself at a decent hour—bed being the couch in the living room since he insisted on being close at hand during the night in case they needed him.

Yes, Claire had had a lot of time to think lying there staring at the ceiling. Time to realize that she had found someone else she could rely on, someone who could help her carry her burdens, a friend she could share her life with. Of course it was too late now, she acknowledged with a hard aching knot in her throat. After all, he'd said himself he'd be crazy to change. Didn't he have the best of both worlds as it was?

Chapter Ten

Agatha Crumbaker was dead and Lieutenant Vincent Pucci knew who did it. But how to prove it? How to prove it was her husband? After all, what reason had Norman to brutally strangle his wife? Agatha had always turned a blind eye on his affair with Constance. Why would he kill Agatha when, with her alive, running his house and taking care of his children, he had the best of both worlds—

David's fingers froze on the keys. Aaagh! He punched repeatedly at the Delete key, making the offending words disappear from the screen with technological magic. He started again—*running his house and taking care of his children, he...he...* He what? Damn! Once again David held the key down, making the cursor race backward through the letters he'd just typed, blinking them into oblivion, leaving not a trace to recriminate him. Now why couldn't he have something like that for his mouth, he asked himself, shoving his chair back from the desk with an impatient push of his arms. Some magic button he could hit that would reverse the sound waves making their way from his mouth, forcing him to swallow them, to choke on their stupidity.

I've got the best of both worlds right here, he'd said. *What man could ask for more?* he'd said. What a fool! David groaned and laid his head back against the top edge of his chair, staring up at the ceiling. It'd been a joke! He'd said the words lightly, without thinking, just a little harmless repartee. He'd been kidding, for God's sake! So how come a guilty flush had started at his neck and hadn't stopped till it was imbedded somewhere in his scalp? How come he'd sat staring at Claire, frozen dumb, and then when, naturally enough, she'd acted hurt and angry, he'd responded with an equal amount of anger?

Guilty conscience, Olson? Are you going to have the guts to admit to yourself that there might have been a grain of truth in those famous last words? David closed his eyes since the ceiling was offering no answers. He tried to concentrate, to sift through the conflicting emotions warring inside him, offering himself motives, justifications, reasons. That last year of their marriage had been rough, no doubt about it. So had he taken the easy way out? Had he been so shallow, so immature, that he'd let Claire go, secretly relieved to be able to stop the struggle, willing to selfishly enjoy the nearness of his wife and child without having to pay the price of—oh, such a painful word—commitment?

You deserve to lose her, you jerk! David opened his eyes. Wearily he inched his chair back up to the desk and placed his fingers on the keyboard. He stared at the computer, his mind as blank as the screen in front of him. He'd never felt less like writing in his life. But what was it the Captain had said? That he had a responsibility to his craft, if nothing else? Responsibility. David took a deep breath and squared his shoulders. By God, this was one commitment he was going to damn well try to fulfill!

Okay. So, Lieutenant Vincent Pucci knew that Agatha's husband had killed her. Now, for the motive. David's fingers began to move quickly over the keys.

By the end of the second week, Claire was feeling almost up to par, physically if not mentally. She still needed a lot of rest, but a nap in the afternoon and an early night were enough to guarantee that she made it through the day in fairly good shape. She'd even started doing a couple of hours of work in the morning. Claire's bout with chicken pox was over, leaving her with only one small scar on her back and a lifelong aversion to chamomile lotion.

So if she was healthy again, why did no one seem to be in any hurry to have David move back upstairs? she asked herself one morning on her way to the shower. Katy was in seventh heaven, making no secret of the fact that she wanted her dad to stay "for never, and never and never." And David acted as though he was settled in for the duration, seemingly perfectly happy to sleep on the couch indefinitely. It looked as if it was up to Claire to do something about the situation.

Of course, she wanted him to stay, too. Although she wasn't happy about him sleeping on the couch—she wanted him in her bed.

Nothing like being blunt, Claire! she chided herself as she finished her quick shower and stared at her blurred reflection in the steamy bathroom mirror. She wanted David back in her bed, back in her life—back, period! And that was just too damned bad, wasn't it? Claire told herself briskly. She dried off with movements as brisk as her thoughts and proceeded to get dressed for the day just as efficiently in jeans and a lightweight sweater. This was going to be her first day back among the living, her first full day out of pajamas and robe—cause for celebration.

Unfortunately she didn't feel much like celebrating. Too bad, too bad, too bad. The words had echoed around her brain for days, a background chant like a mantra, numbing her to what she saw as an almost comic irony. It was just too ironic that she had spent so much energy these past months fobbing off David's attempts at a reconciliation, while now that she no longer wanted to "fob," David no longer wanted to reconcile.

Oh, he probably hadn't realized it yet, Claire knew, going into the kitchen to make herself some toast and pour a glass of juice. It would be hard for him to admit that all his endless badgering had become no more than a sort of routine between them—a stock standard in his repertoire of charm. The truth was, David didn't want her back as his wife. His words about having the best of both worlds had simply rung too true. At the time, he might not have known he meant them—but he had.

And then there was the simple matter of love. Claire paused in the middle of spreading butter on a piece of toast, her knife stilling, allowing its curl of golden butter to melt and pool in the center of the bread. David had never, *never*—even in the middle of one of his flowery speeches proclaiming their "rightness" together—mentioned the word love. He'd never said that he'd never stopped loving her or that he suddenly found himself loving her again. Never.

Claire let the knife clatter to the counter, breakfast forgotten. It was time to end this ridiculous farce their divorce had become! Having David as some sort of pseudohusband was just too painful. Maybe she should persuade him to move to New York, after all. She couldn't go on loving a half husband in a half marriage any longer.

And the first step was to get him out of her house—again.

Claire made her way down the hall to her office, her back so stiff with resolution it was reflected in her gait, she barely bent her knees as she walked. She rapped on the door with the back of her knuckles, already turning the knob without waiting for a reply.

David didn't appear to hear her or notice her approach. He was hunched over the keyboard, fingers flying, his face mere inches from the lighted computer screen as if proximity could somehow speed the flow of words from his brain to the computer.

"David?" Even though she said the words quietly, he jumped, startled. He looked up at her with unfocused eyes, obviously still deep in his story.

"David, it's time for you to go."

"Huh?"

"Home, David. It's time for you to go home, move back upstairs." She tried to add "maybe move to New York," but the words seemed to stick in her throat. She found herself swallowing convulsively.

"Huh?"

Claire expelled a breath with exasperated force. "Are you listening to me? David?" She waited for a look of self-recognition to sharpen his eyes, waited for the series of blinks that told her he was once again David Olson instead of Lieutenant Vincent Pucci, hard-boiled detective with a passion for pasta.

"Are you with me now? I was telling you that I'm fit and healthy and can take care of things around here again. You should go ahead and move your stuff upstairs today."

David was shaking his head. "I don't think it'd be a good idea to leave you here alone yet, sweetheart. When you're recuperating you really need the company."

"Company! Company's the last thing I need!"

"Hmm, I suppose so," David conceded. "You certainly haven't lacked visitors at your sickbed, have you?"

In fact, Claire had had an almost constant stream of friends and family stopping by to entertain her. Naomi had come by everyday for a chat or to play with Katy, and even the Captain had taken to showing up, his box of pewter soldiers tucked under his arm, stating gruffly that there was nothing like a good battle to take her mind off her itching. She couldn't say they talked much, but she had to admit, it was a fascinating game. And her mother, with her oranges, was a daily visitor. Truthfully Claire was looking forward to the peace and quiet of health—company was the last thing she needed and she said as much to David.

"Well, if I can't stay for altruistic reasons then I've got to stay for selfish reasons. I'm on a roll! I can't leave yet, I'm doing some great work here. It must be your aura or something." He gave her a pleased smile as he shared his news. "I sent off a revised chapter and new outline to my editor—sort of a compromise between his ideas and mine—and he thought it was great! And I think it's semigreat so it looks like things are going to happen with the old Lieutenant after all— he's got the green light and we're ready to go!"

"Well, I'm glad, David, but—" Ready to go? The association hit Claire like a thunderbolt. The tour! She'd known she'd been forgetting something important! He'd missed his book tour!

"David, you missed your tour! Your four-city, autograph-party, free-hors-d'oeuvres, loads-of-publicity book tour!" Claire was horrified. David adored the limelight; he was in his element at such things. How could he have—

But David was shrugging his shoulders. "Barney's trying to reschedule it. Lord, Claire, you didn't think I was just going to walk out on you when you were so sick, did you?"

"Yes! I mean you should have! I mean I wanted you to!" Claire was stricken. He'd canceled his promotional tour to stay with her! But she'd told him to go! Well, maybe not directly, but she distinctly remembered telling him that he didn't have to take care of her. Yet he didn't go. Claire was dumbstruck by the parallel between now and two years ago. She'd told him to go then, and he'd left. She told him to go now—and he stayed.

Claire's resolve to get David out of her life disappeared from her mind without so much as a last gasp of mental struggle. It didn't stand a chance in the face of the powerful new determination that surged into her brain, one that demanded she get him back in her life—for good! She loved him and she couldn't bear to lose him again! She'd just have to make him see that he *didn't* have the best of both worlds the way things stood now—that the best of *all* worlds was waiting for him with her and Katy. But how to get him to see that? How to approach it? *Oh, by the way, you know the way you've been talking about getting together again—well, do you want an indoor or outdoor wedding?*

"So I need to stay a couple more days, okay?" David's voice interrupted her chaotic thoughts. He was staring at her oddly. "Okay, Claire? It'll give you a chance to ease back into the old routine slowly, won't be such a shock to your system. You don't want to overdo things. Okay?"

"Fine," Claire managed to say, backing toward the door. "Sure." She fairly fled from the office, her mind working at whirlwind speed.

How in God's name did you make someone fall in love with you twice!

She was still pondering, rejecting scenario after scenario, when her mother stopped by.

"Grandma's here!" Katy shouted, running to open the door. "What'd you bring me?" Claire heard her demand.

"No, sweetie, these are for your mother," she heard, followed by the sound of footsteps starting down the hallway toward the bedrooms.

"I'm in here, Mom," Claire called from the living room where she was trying to sort through two weeks worth of mail that had piled up while she was ill.

"Are you sure you should be up?" Anna Edwards clucked, following the sound of her daughter's voice. "All that junk mail can wait till you're stronger, can't it?"

Claire pushed aside a stack of flyers piled next to her on the couch and made room for her mother to sit down. "This isn't exactly manual labor. I think I'm up to a little envelope slitting."

"I brought you some oranges," Anna said needlessly, dropping the sack onto the coffee table.

Claire smiled her thanks, not having the heart to admit to her mother that she was about as sick of oranges as she was of chamomile lotion.

"Katy, add these to the fruit bowl in the kitchen, would you please," Claire asked, handing her daughter the brown paper sack and sending her skipping out of the room.

"You still need the Vitamin C, you know," Anna admonished. "And I read somewhere that fresh Vitamin C does you a lot more good than those vitamin pills. Probably cheaper in the long run, too. Although, can you believe it, oranges are $1.19 a pound! Supposed to be some freeze in Florida. Or Texas. I don't remember."

Not that again! "Would you like me to pay you back for them?" Claire offered, keeping her tone mild.

"Heavens no!" Her mother sounded shocked to the core.

"When you mentioned how much they were—that really is outrageous—I thought maybe it was too much..."

"Darling, I just thought you'd be interested, that's all!"

Her mother's feathers had definitely been ruffled by her suggestion so Claire hastened to change the subject, turning the talk to Katy, Grandma's favorite topic. But Claire found her mind dwelling on her mother's comments; she couldn't let the matter drop so easily. Some reminiscence of her mother's about how much Katy was like Claire when she was a child gave Claire the opening she was looking for. "Mom, was money really tight with you and Dad when I was little?"

"Oh, I don't know. No, not really." Anna Edwards paused for a moment, considering. "Oh, I guess we had a few lean years there when Momma was sick. Remember when she lived with us? But it wasn't too bad. Not like when *I* was a girl!" She sighed. "Of course, that was during the depression and Momma had so many of us to try to feed and clothe and there was *no* money. Money, money, money—that's all she ever talked about! Momma was a tired old woman by the time she was forty, worn-out worrying about money. So compared to her I've had it pretty easy, I'd say. Now today's kids? Well, that's a whole other ball game, I tell you what! I walked by that toy store in the mall the other day, and..."

But Claire wasn't really paying attention to her mother's story. She was struck by the fact that Anna Edwards had no idea of the legacy she'd inherited from her mother. Or that Claire could have used the very same words to describe Anna as Anna had used to describe her mother. And, until very recently, Claire suspected that Katy would have found it an apt description of Claire. She became more determined than ever to be sure that this was one family trait that wasn't passed down to the next generation.

She tried to pull her thoughts back to her mother's words but Anna had noticed her distraction. "Darling, are you sure you're feeling better?" she was asking. "You still look a little pale—sort of droopy."

In the face of her mother's concern, all other thoughts flew from her mind and Claire suddenly found her lower lip beginning to quiver and, out of the blue, tears were pricking her eyes.

Immediately an arm was around her shoulder and a voice was crooning softly. "What is it, sweetie? What's the matter?"

That was her undoing. It was as if a dam had burst and the words spilled from her. "Oh, Mom! I still love David! I want him back! What should I do?" She couldn't stop the tears from overflowing down her cheeks.

To her surprise, Anna didn't look surprised—more relieved than anything else. "Is that all?" she asked with a hint of a smile. "I'd say the simplest thing to do would be to tell the poor boy and put him out of his misery."

"But he doesn't love me!" Claire wailed.

Now her mother did look surprised. "Where did you *ever* get an idea like that?"

Claire pulled away, sitting up straighter, still sniffling. "He likes it better the way it is now, where he doesn't have all the pressures and problems of marriage."

"So that's why he's spent the last two weeks nursing you? Why he's hardly left your side? He was looking for the easy, no-pressure way out?" Her mother stroked back her long hair. "Baby, baby, I've watched you two play this ridiculous divorce game of yours for two years now, with neither one of you acting the least bit divorced—" She held up a hand to stop the protest that sprang to Claire's lips. "I know, I know, you've both pretended to see other people but it was all pure window-dressing. I, for one, will be thrilled when you put an end to all this nonsense and start living as man and wife legally and physically, since you never stopped mentally!"

Claire was floored by her mother's words, even while realizing that she was right. She had no more accepted the divorce than David had; she'd just been a little more adept at fooling herself! Claire threw her arms around her mother and hugged her. What a dear, wise, wonderful woman! It was time to put a stop to this "nonsense." Tonight. They put their heads together and started planning. David Olson might not know it yet, but he was a married man!

The pot roast was a little dry—Claire had been having trouble concentrating and she'd left it in the oven a bit too long—and the gravy had one or two lumps in it. But the new potatoes and peas were perfect and you could hardly go wrong with ice cream for dessert. All in all, Claire was pleased with her evening's performance, and if David was a little suspicious by her sudden desire to prepare a special meal and by Grandma's unexpected offer to have Katy stay overnight—well, he didn't say anything.

Claire was surprised he didn't question her on her nervousness, though. She was fairly jumping out of her skin, anticipating yet dreading what she was about to do. And she couldn't keep her mind on their conversation, since a separate conversation was running simultaneously through her brain, one where she laid her heart and soul bare for his acceptance or refusal. No wonder he kept repeating everything twice.

"Claire? Claire? I asked if you wanted more coffee." They were still seated across from each other at the dinner table, dessert bowls pushed aside, sipping coffee.

"No, thanks. No more." Shifting uneasily in her chair, Claire reached out and began to fidget with the bowl of fruit in the middle of the table, picking up and putting down one orange after another. "Do you know how much this orange cost?" she asked suddenly, holding it up, examining it this way and that under the light as if it were some alien object.

"Not a clue."

"I do. And my mother does—to the cent. And I can bet her mother would have known. Give Katy another five years, and the way things were going, she would have known, too." Claire stared at him across the table, eyes very serious. "David, I promise you, I will do my very best to be sure Katy never knows the exact cost of an orange."

"Claire, what are you talking about?"

Stumbling, haltingly, Claire began to talk, telling him about oranges, about her grandmother, about The Note.

"David, I know the last year or so of our marriage I was impossible to live with. Nagging and worrying. And I know I'm the one who said that stuff about a leopard not being able to change its spots—but, damn it, I *have* changed!" She paused, then suddenly insisted, as if he were about to argue with her, "And *you've* changed! Although I don't think I'd care anymore if you'd changed or not. Or what you drive. Or whether you go to Alaska—which is a hell of a lot better than Korea or Vietnam—"

"Wait! Wait a minute!" David held up a hand, trying to stop the ever-quickening flow of words. "Claire, is there a point to this story? Could it be possible that this rambling of yours is a way of telling me—that you love me?"

Claire swallowed. Hard. She managed to nod her head.

"And did you cook me pot roast tonight to prove to me that you've changed?"

Claire nodded again.

"And since I ate your pot roast, what does that mean?"

"I have absolutely no idea," Claire said, but a smile was beginning to curve her lips, her face reflecting the glow that had started in David's eyes.

"Well, given the state of that pot roast, I'd say it obviously means I love you, too. And that I still intend to do all the cooking when we get back from our second honeymoon."

"Now, that sounds like the best of both worlds to me!" Claire said teasingly, somehow finding herself on the other side of the table, sitting on his lap with her arms around his neck and his own hugging almost fiercely, possessively, around her waist.

"Don't joke about that, Claire!" David groaned. "I can't believe you've forgiven me for that." He hesitated, hating to ask, "You know—you know that it was sort of true—just a little bit true, don't you?"

Claire nodded. "I didn't think *you* knew it was true."

"Well, it wasn't something I liked admitting but, unfortunately, I seemed to have picked up this bad habit of self-awareness lately."

"That's okay," Claire told him, laying her head against his shoulder. "Because I've decided I sort of like spending money."

Her laughter joined David's until their lips found something better, quieter, to do.

* * *

The wedding was outdoors in the backyard of the old, three-story house. Naomi Maxwell was the matron of honor and her husband, Sam, splendid in his decorated captain's uniform, was best man. The bride wore a sea-green dress of layer upon layer of gauzy material that floated around her ankles like foam, a wreath of white blossoms circling her crown of dark hair. The groom, although rather pale from his two weeks in a darkened bedroom and with the remains of a small scab on his cheek, was still rakishly handsome in his gray tuxedo and rainbow-striped suspenders.

"Are you still itching, Daddy?" the little flower girl asked, standing between the bride and groom as they greeted their guests after the ceremony.

"Not too bad," David replied, "but maybe you could scratch right there in the middle—up a little—over—the other way—perfect." He sighed as little fingers found the right spot on his back.

"I'm so glad you didn't have to postpone the wedding," Naomi said, approaching on her husband's arm to give both bride and groom a hug and kiss. "I mean, chicken pox might be a good enough reason to cancel a school field trip—but a wedding! No one would ever believe it."

"I can't believe I had to suffer through them twice!" David replied with a grin. "But the doctor said sometimes if you have a really mild case as an infant, it doesn't give you lifetime immunity."

"As sick as you were this time you should be immune for several lifetimes," Claire said, suppressing a small shudder. "I don't think I could go through the worry again."

"If you intend to fill up this big old house with kids like you said you were, then you're going to have to go through chicken pox a half-dozen times or more," the Captain pointed out practically.

"Don't remind me!" Claire laughed, but then sobered, smiling fondly at her two friends. "And don't remind me that you're going to be moving, either. I was just getting good enough to capture one of your battalions every once in a while!" The Maxwells had decided to stay in the Minneapolis area after all and were in the process of buying a house near their daughter, pointing out that Claire and David would need the extra floors once they were a family again.

"Oh, there you two are!" Anna Edwards came up behind them. "Uncle Ralph wants to get some pictures now. Over by that tree there. Come on, come on." She shooed them ahead of her. "I'm so glad you decided to use Ralph for your photographer. One of those studio places charges an arm and a leg! You were so smart to keep it small and outside—weddings can be outrageously expensive! Why, by the time you add up the caterer, the dress, the invitations—the first time around you almost bankrupted us! I remember—"

Claire and David exchanged smiling glances, letting her mother's words flow over and around them. Claire could accept and love her mother the way she was, even if she was grateful she had broken the mold herself.

"David!" A small, balding man in a neat suit and ugly striped tie halted them, hurrying over with quick, birdlike steps to shake David's hand. "Chicken pox! Weddings! Honeymoons! When are you going to run out of excuses for putting off my tour? Your public wants you, they need you, they love you!''

David laughed, patting the little man on the back. "Next month, I promise!" He introduced Claire. "Darling, this is Barney, my agent. Barney, this is Claire—my friend.''

Claire smiled a greeting, startled at David's choice of words. As her mother continued ushering them over to the waiting photographer, Claire said in a low voice, ''It's okay to say wife, now, you know.'' She was thinking of the time when she'd scolded him for introducing her to his date as his wife.

''I know,'' David replied, taking her hand, his eyes holding hers, blocking out the noise and confusion around them. ''But you've always been my wife, Claire. Now I want the whole world to know how proud I am that you're also my friend.''

They posed under the crab-apple tree that was just losing the last of its bright blossoms, dropping them to the grass to make a soft pink carpet under their feet. Claire looked up overhead at its branches, just beginning to leaf out in the green miracle of spring, of rebirth, of joyous love, then she reached out to pat the thick bark of the trunk—as old and gnarled and eternal looking as friendship.

*　*　*　*　*

Silhouette

SPECIAL EDITION™

VOWS
A series celebrating marriage
by Sherryl Woods

To Love, Honor and Cherish—these were the words that three
generations of Halloran men promised their women they'd live
by. But these vows made in love are each challenged by the
tests of time....

In October—Jason Halloran meets his match in *Love* #769;
In November—Kevin Halloran rediscovers love—with his
wife—in *Honor* #775;
In December—Brandon Halloran rekindles an old flame in
Cherish #781.

These three stirring tales are coming down the aisle toward
you—only from Silhouette Special Edition!

If you missed the first VOWS title, *Love* (SE #769), order your copy now by sending your name,
address, zip or postal code, along with a check or money order (please do not send cash)
for $3.39 for each book ordered, plus 75¢ postage and handling ($1.00 in Canada), payable
to Silhouette Books, to:

In the U.S.

Silhouette Books
3010 Walden Avenue
P.O. Box 1396
Buffalo, NY 14269-1396

In Canada

Silhouette Books
P.O. Box 609
Fort Erie, Ontario
L2A 5X3

Please specify book title with your order.
Canadian residents add applicable federal and provincial taxes.

SESW-2

Take 4 bestselling love stories FREE

Plus get a FREE surprise gift!

Special Limited-time Offer

Mail to Silhouette Reader Service™

In the U.S.	In Canada
3010 Walden Avenue	P.O. Box 609
P.O. Box 1867	Fort Erie, Ontario
Buffalo, N.Y. 14269-1867	L2A 5X3

YES! Please send me 4 free Silhouette Romance™ novels and my free surprise gift. Then send me 6 brand-new novels every month, which I will receive months before they appear in bookstores. Bill me at the low price of $2.25* each—a savings of 44¢ apiece off the cover prices. There are no shipping, handling or other hidden costs. I understand that accepting the books and gift places me under no obligation ever to buy any books. I can always return a shipment and cancel at any time. Even if I never buy another book from Silhouette, the 4 free books and the surprise gift are mine to keep forever.

*Offer slightly different in Canada—$2.25 per book plus 69¢ per shipment for delivery. Canadian residents add applicable federal and provincial sales tax. Sales tax applicable in N.Y.

215 BPA ADL9   315 BPA ADMN

Name _____ (PLEASE PRINT)

Address _____ Apt. No. _____

City _____ State/Prov. _____ Zip/Postal Code. _____

This offer is limited to one order per household and not valid to present Silhouette Romance™ subscribers. Terms and prices are subject to change.

SROM-92   © 1990 Harlequin Enterprises Limited

Silhouette
R O M A N C E™

HEARTLAND HOLIDAYS

Christmas bells turn into wedding bells for the Gallagher siblings in Stella Bagwell's *Heartland Holidays* trilogy.

THEIR FIRST THANKSGIVING (#903) in November
Olivia Westcott had once rejected Sam Gallagher's proposal—and in his stubborn pride, he'd refused to hear her reasons why. Now Olivia is back...and it is about time Sam Gallagher listened!

THE BEST CHRISTMAS EVER (#909) in December
Soldier Nick Gallagher had come home to be the best man at his brother's wedding—not to be a groom! But when he met single mother Allison Lee, he knew he'd found his bride.

NEW YEAR'S BABY (#915) in January
Kathleen Gallagher had given up on love and marriage until she came to the rescue of neighbor Ross Douglas . . . and the newborn baby he'd found on his doorstep!

Come celebrate the holidays with Silhouette Romance!

Available at your favorite retail outlet, or order your copy now by sending your name, address, zip or postal code, along with a check or money order for $2.69 for each book ordered (please do not send cash), plus 75¢ postage and handling ($1.00 in Canada), payable to Silhouette Books to:

In the U.S.
3010 Walden Avenue
P.O. Box 1396
Buffalo, NY 14269-1396

In Canada
P.O. Box 609
Fort Erie, Ontario
L2A 5X3

Please specify book title(s) with your order.
Canadian residents add applicable federal and provincial taxes.

HEART1

Silhouette

CHRISTMAS

Stories
1992

Experience the beauty of Yuletide romance with Silhouette
Christmas Stories 1992—a collection of heartwarming stories by
favorite Silhouette authors.

JONI'S MAGIC by Mary Lynn Baxter
HEARTS OF HOPE by Sondra Stanford
THE NIGHT SANTA CLAUS RETURNED by Marie Ferrarrella
BASKET OF LOVE by Jeanne Stephens

Also available this year are three popular early editions of
Silhouette Christmas Stories—1986, 1987 and 1988. Look for
these and you'll be well on your way to a complete collection
of the best in holiday romance.

Plus, as an added bonus, you can receive a FREE keepsake
Christmas ornament. Just collect four proofs of purchase from
any November or December 1992 Harlequin or Silhouette series
novels, or from any Harlequin or Silhouette Christmas
collection, and receive a beautiful dated brass Christmas
candle ornament.

Mail this certificate along with four (4) proof-of-purchase coupons, plus $1.50 postage and
handling (check or money order—do not send cash), payable to Silhouette Books, to: **In the
U.S.:** P.O. Box 9057, Buffalo, NY 14269-9057; **In Canada:** P.O. Box 622, Fort Erie, Ontario,
L2A 5X3.

**ONE PROOF OF
PURCHASE**

SX92POP

Name: _____

_____

Address: _____

_____

City: _____

State/Province: _____

Zip/Postal Code: _____

093 KAG